Thread Reckoning

AN EMBROIDERY MYSTERY

AMANDA LEE

AN OBSIDIAN MYSTERY

OBSIDIAN
Published by New American Library, a division of
Penguin Group (USA) Inc., 375 Hudson Street,
New York, New York 10014, USA
Penguin Group (Canada), 90 Eglinton Avenue East, Suite 700, Toronto,
Ontario M4P 2Y3, Canada (a division of Pearson Penguin Canada Inc.)
Penguin Books Ltd., 80 Strand, London WC2R 0RL, England
Penguin Ireland, 25 St. Stephen's Green, Dublin 2,
Ireland (a division of Penguin Books Ltd.)
Penguin Group (Australia), 250 Camberwell Road, Camberwell, Victoria 3124,
Australia (a division of Pearson Australia Group Pty. Ltd.)
Penguin Books India Pvt. Ltd., 11 Community Centre, Panchsheel Park,
New Delhi - 110 017, India
Penguin Group (NZ), 67 Apollo Drive, Rosedale, Auckland 0632,
New Zealand (a division of Pearson New Zealand Ltd.)
Penguin Books (South Africa) (Pty.) Ltd., 24 Sturdee Avenue,
Rosebank, Johannesburg 2196, South Africa

Penguin Books Ltd., Registered Offices:
80 Strand, London WC2R 0RL, England

First published by Obsidian, an imprint of New American Library,
a division of Penguin Group (USA) Inc.

First Printing, September 2011
10 9 8 7 6 5 4 3 2 1

Printed in the United States of America

PRAISE FOR THE EMBROIDERY MYSTERY SERIES

Stitch Me Deadly

"The writing is lively. . . . This book should appeal not only to embroidery enthusiasts, antique-hunters, and dog lovers, but to anyone who likes a smartly written cozy."

—Fresh Fiction

The Quick and the Thread

"Lee kicks off a cozy, promising mystery series . . . a fast, pleasant read with prose full of pop culture references and, of course, sharp needlework puns."

—*Publishers Weekly*

"In her debut novel, *The Quick and the Thread*, author Amanda Lee gives her Embroidery Mystery series a rousing start with a fast-paced, intriguing who-done-it that will delight fans of the cozy mystery genre."

—Fresh Fiction

"Stands out with its likable characters and polished plot."

—The Mystery Reader

"If her debut here is any indication, Lee's new series is going to be fun, spunky, and educational. She smoothly interweaves plot with her [main] character's personality and charm, while dropping tantalizing hints of stitching projects and their history. Marcy Singer is young, fun, sharp, and likable. Readers will be looking forward to her future adventures."

—*Romantic Times*

Also by Amanda Lee

The Quick and the Thread
Stitch Me Deadly

For Caleb, Carlie, Nicholas, Jennica, Andrew, Faith, Nathan, Lexi, Daniel, Grace, Jake, Lindsey, Rachel, and Logan

Special thanks to my 2010 Teach Blountville creative writing class—you guys rock! In addition, I'd like to thank the incomparable Jessica Wade, Robert Gottlieb, Kim Lionetti, and Kaitlyn Kennedy. As always, thanks so much to Tim, Lianna, and Nicholas for your love and support.

Chapter One

It was your typical Tuesday at the Seven-Year Stitch, insofar as there's ever *anything* typical about Tallulah Falls. Since February is both Black History Month and the month when nearby Lincoln City hosts its weeklong antiques festival, I was sitting in my favorite red chair in the sit-and-stitch square working on a quilt in the tradition of the Congolese Kuba cloth that I was hoping to display at the festival. My quilt was a camel color, with a design of intertwining diamonds.

Funny that I was stitching diamonds at that particular moment. The bells over the door jingled, and I looked up to see a stunning young woman entering the shop with a clear garment bag over her shoulder. The garment bag contained an ivory wedding dress. Thus, the coincidence about my embroidering diamonds, see?

Angus, my lanky Irish wolfhound, loped over to greet the woman. The horror in her eyes, combined with the fact that she was backing up as fast as her long, lean legs would carry her, led me to believe she might not be a dog person.

"Angus," I called, laying aside my Kuba cloth carefully. Kuba cloths are believed to have originated in the Congo sometime before the beginning of the sixteenth century. I loved the version I was working on.

Angus immediately trotted to my side. I instructed him to sit and to stay. Those obedience classes I'd enrolled him in when he was still only a few months old were paying off big-time right now.

"Sorry about that," I said to the customer. "I'm Marcy Singer. How can I help you today?"

"Well, I was going to ask you to do some embroidery work for me," the woman said, her hazel eyes still watching Angus warily. "But this is a very delicate gown—it was my mother's—and I can't leave it here. I'm afraid that . . . that dog . . . will ruin it."

"I can assure you I'll take excellent care of the dress." I stepped behind the counter and got Angus' leash. "In fact, let me put him in the back while we discuss the work you'd like done."

Although he hates it, Angus' private little room at the shop is the bathroom. I put him there when there's someone in the store who is nervous around him or who has a delicate condition—particularly frail, elderly people, toddlers, and pregnant women come to mind. He has a water bowl and a couple toys in there, but he's never a happy camper when he's sent to "his room."

"It'll only be for a few minutes," I whispered as I ushered the whining dog inside and closed the door.

When I returned to the shop area, the woman—who appeared to be in her midtwenties—was sweeping her brown curls off her forehead. Her hair had been professionally highlighted with blond streaks, and these streaks caught the sun that was peeping through the clouds and through the window.

"Is he here all the time?" she asked.

"Most of the time," I said. "Although I do let him stay home on pretty days."

"We don't get many of those on the coast in February."

I laughed. "Nope. Of the four days we've had this month, it's rained three." I nodded toward the garment bag. "What sort of embroidery did you have in mind for the dress?"

"Is he shedding?" she asked, eyes darting to the navy sofa behind me.

"Not at the moment, but I'll be happy to get a lint brush and go over the sofa if you'd like me to."

"Yes, please."

Smiling but gritting my teeth, I retrieved the lint brush from beneath the counter and went over both the navy sofas and the two red chairs that form the square seating area. After I'd finished delinting the furniture, I followed her gaze around the shop. She eyed the black-and-white-checkered tile that covered the floor to the right of the seating area, the maple bins containing yarn and embroidery flosses, and the examples of my work displayed on the walls and shelves.

"What's with the dummy?" she asked as I returned the lint brush to the counter.

I explained that Jill—the mannequin who bears a striking resemblance to Marilyn Monroe and who stands near the cash register, and who today was wearing a jaunty red hat and scarf upon which I'd cross-stitched snowmen—was sort of the shop mascot.

"The Seven-Year Stitch . . . a takeoff on the movie *The Seven-Year Itch*," I said. "Get it?"

"I thought the dog was the mascot."

"Well, you can't ever have too many mascots, can you?"

She shrugged and at last opened the garment bag and spread the wedding gown across the sofa facing away from the window. Once it was outside the bag, I could see that the gown wasn't the gasp-inducing creation I'd hoped it was. Apparently, it wasn't too pleasing to the bride-to-be, either, or else she wouldn't be here, wanting me to embellish it.

"As you can see, the dress has some yellowing here near the neckline and a little around the hem," she said. "It wasn't stored properly or something."

There was some significant yellowing on the bodice, especially near the neckline, so that would take quite a bit of work to cover up. I could also see where there would need to be embroidered lace or perhaps ribbon embroidery all around the hem as well.

"I see definite possibilities," I said. "Are you wanting something elaborate or more subtle?"

"Elaborate. My mother-in-law is providing some pearls, crystals, and some other kinds of gems she thinks might look nice on the dress. So I'll want elaborate, just not tacky."

I smiled. "I can handle that."

"Could you sketch out some design ideas that I could stop back by and look at tomorrow?"

"I sure can. Would you mind if I take a photo of the gown with my phone so I can use it for the designs?"

"That'll be fine," she said.

"Would you hold the dress up in front of you?"

With a sigh of impatience, the woman complied with my request. "I'm Cassandra Wainwright, by the way."

"It's nice to meet you." I snapped the photograph. "I'll work on the designs today and see what I can come up with. Can you tell me about how large the gems are?"

Cassandra shrugged. "All sizes. There are both larger and smaller pearls. The crystals are pretty uniform in size, and they're—I don't know—about a third of a carat maybe? Then she has a few sapphire-looking gems that are at least two carats apiece."

"What do the pearls look like?" I asked. "Are they freshwater or saltwater?"

"Um . . . they're round."

"Saltwater," I said.

"And they're probably not actual pearls," Cassandra said. "My mother-in-law doesn't make that much money. In fact, she lost her job a while back and had to move here. I'm afraid she's going to wind up living with us, because I'm not even sure she qualified for her pension." She waved her hand. "But back to the dress. If I like the designs you come up with, I'll give you a retainer and we'll go from there. Provided I do hire you, I'd like you to start on the dress right away. My fiancé and I are getting married on Valentine's Day."

Nothing like loads of notice, I thought. "No problem," I said.

Cassandra put the gown back in the garment bag and said she and her fiancé would be back tomorrow to look at my designs. I hurried to let Angus out of the bathroom as soon as she left.

I was thinking most women select their wedding dress on their own . . . or with their mother or their best friend. To me, it was unusual for Cassandra to include her fiancé in the dress design. Who knows? Maybe she was marrying a fashion designer.

When I'd almost gotten married a few years ago, I certainly hadn't included David when I'd chosen my dress. My dress had been gorgeous—prettier than the plain ivory gown Cassandra had brought in. Mom had designed it, of course. My mother is Beverly Singer, a costume designer to many Hollywood A-listers. She'd done several wedding gowns for movies, but this was her first "real" gown. And since it was for her only child, she planned to go all out. And since I planned to be married only once, I let her.

We looked through one wedding magazine after another until I found two gowns I thought—or rather knew—Mom could combine into the one perfect gown. And she did. The bodice had a sweetheart neckline with silver metallic embroidery and intricate beadwork. The full organza skirt had a sweep train with beading that echoed and enhanced the beadwork on the bodice. At the waist was a cluster of pearls and crystals that looked like an ornate brooch.

I knew that it would absolutely blow David away. And it might have . . . if he'd ever seen it. He didn't show up at the wedding. The best man,

Sadie, Blake, and Mom were all calling everywhere. Mom was convinced David had been in some sort of accident. Sadie and Blake didn't say anything that day, but they were thinking what I was thinking—the truth—that David had gotten cold feet.

The best man, Tony, was able to get in touch with David about an hour after the ceremony was to have started. He had been David's best friend all through college and knew of a dive where David liked to hang out and drink. I was in the garden alone—still wearing the wedding gown—when Tony approached me. I remember how the wind was blowing my hair and how the gown was billowing, and I was thinking what a shame it was that there would be no wedding pictures and that no one would be able to admire this beautiful gown Mom had poured so much of herself into.

"You know, he could've called me yesterday," I'd said to Tony.

He'd bowed his head.

"Or even this morning. Actually, anytime before the guests got here would have been nice." I knew Tony wasn't to blame—after all, he'd shown up for the wedding—but I also knew David would ask Tony what I'd had to say.

Tony simply nodded. "He said everything just happened too fast and that it dawned on him that he wasn't ready for marriage."

As tears burned my eyes, I'd turned away from

Tony. He put his hands on my shoulders, but I didn't turn back toward him. I didn't want to fall into his arms and weep. I didn't want to give David the satisfaction of knowing he'd hurt me that badly.

"He wants to know if he can call you tomorrow."

"We have nothing to say to each other," I said.

"He thinks the two of you could still have a future . . . someday."

I'd shaken my head. "Tell him we have nothing . . . and not to ever call me again."

And he didn't. At least, so far he hadn't. It hadn't been forever yet. But I wasn't expecting to ever hear from him again.

Shortly after the breakup, I adopted Angus. That had been over a year ago, but Mom still believed I left San Francisco to avoid running into David or any of our mutual friends. Maybe that was part of it, but I was happy with my new life here in Tallulah Falls . . . for the most part. I'd had my share of bad luck—beginning with finding the man who had leased the shop before me dead on my storeroom floor the first week I was in business. But I'd met a lot of terrific people, business was going well, and my embroidery classes were full every Tuesday, Wednesday, and Thursday evening.

I'd even started dating again. Sadie had fixed me up with Todd Calloway, who owned the Brew Crew, a craft brewery next door. Todd was handsome, witty, charming . . . and he had chocolate brown eyes and a voice that could make you go weak in the knees. We'd been on a few dates.

I'd also been on a couple dates with Detective Ted Nash, who'd investigated the murder of the man found in my storeroom. Our first date was way after that investigation had ended. Ted was handsome, too. He had black hair with some premature gray threaded throughout. It made him look distinguished. Of course, he was a pretty distinguished guy, so the look worked for him.

I was trying to play it cool with both guys at this point rather than rush into a relationship with either one. Todd was recovering from a bad breakup when I met him, and Ted had been through a divorce. And, of course, you know about all the heartache that wedding dress drummed up from my own past.

Putting those thoughts firmly aside, I stepped into my office and booted up the computer. I checked my e-mail first and was pleased to see there was a message from Reggie with photos attached. Reggie Singh was the local librarian, and her husband, Manu, was the sheriff. They were vacationing for two weeks in their native India. They were staying with family in Gujarat, and Reggie had passed along some fantastic photos of her and Manu at the Laxmi Vilas Palace.

Smiling to myself, I sent a note back to Reggie telling her not to let Manu get too comfortable in the palace.

Next thing you know, he'll want to install a throne similar to the raja's in your living room! Seriously, the palace is gorgeous. Enjoy it . . . but come home soon. I miss you guys! We all do.

I printed out the photographs to share with the other members of Reggie's embroidery class. They'd be happy to see she and Manu were having such a good time.

I then uploaded the wedding dress photo to my computer. The dress was a simple sleeveless A-line gown. I enlarged the picture, so I could add embellishments using drawing software. Cassandra didn't seem to be the easiest person in the world to please, so I wanted to give her more than one example.

In the first example, I placed pink silk ribbon rosettes and pastel green ribbon leaves at two-inch intervals along the hem of the dress. I added seed pearls to the upper portion of the skirt. To pull the skirt and bodice together—and to hide the significant yellowing on the bodice—I covered the bodice in pearls and made a more elaborate embroidery ribbon flower and leaf design at the waist that incorporated the crystals. I printed this photograph, saved the file as "Look One," and gave the dress another go.

With the second example, I used the pearls and crystals to make triangular shapes from the hem to about seven inches up the skirt all around. At the top of each triangle, I placed one of the sapphire gems Cassandra had mentioned. To adorn the bodice this time, I used the crystals, the pearls, and one large sapphire at the top center of the bodice. This design, of course, would depend on how many "gems" Cassandra's mother-in-law was bringing to the table. I printed and saved "Look Two."

Before I could begin "Look Three," the bells over the door jingled, letting me know someone was in the shop. I helped the customer—a middle-aged woman with a cheery disposition—find the cross-stitch pattern she was looking for, and then I wandered around looking for embroidery books that might help me decide how to approach "Look Three." The two designs I'd already come up with were about the best I could do. I was pretty pleased with them, admittedly. And I needed to keep the design simple enough that I'd be able to finish it in time for Cassandra's Valentine's Day wedding.

I took two books featuring embroidery designs on clothing and sat down on the sofa facing the window. I opened the top book and began thumbing through it. Naturally, instead of seeing anything for the wedding dress, I saw things that would beautifully accentuate some of my own clothes.

Angus got up and walked to the door—the indicator that he needed to go outside. I set the books aside, grabbed Angus' leash off the counter, and placed the clock sign on the door that promised I'd be back in five minutes. Angus hurried down the stone walk to the wrought-iron clock standing in the shopping center square. As we jogged past the aromatherapy shop, I happened to glance inside. Nellie Davis, the proprietor, can't stand me, so I have no idea what prompted me to peek into her shop window. But what I saw made me stop in my tracks, causing Angus to nearly pull me off my feet.

I saw David.

Yes, the David. David who left me at the altar. David whom I'd never have dreamed I'd see in Tallulah Falls, Oregon.

I quickly regained my balance and followed Angus to the square. Sometimes extend-a-leashes are terrific. Sometimes not so much. I wanted to take another look into that shop or see who walked out of it without being terribly obvious. I was almost certain my eyes were playing tricks on me, because Cassandra and her wedding dress had dredged up emotions I'd been trying to tamp down for so long. But I wanted to be absolutely certain my eyes were playing tricks.

As Angus sniffed around the grass, I watched the shop. The man who came out turned so quickly that I couldn't get a good look at his face. But he had the same sandy blond hair as David. He was the same height . . . had the same build . . . walked the same way.

"No way," I whispered. "Please let me be wrong about this."

If it was David and his being in Tallulah Falls was more than a mere coincidence—if he was here to see me—he'd stop at the Seven-Year Stitch. Right? But this guy strolled right on by without a second glance at the shop. It couldn't be David. It couldn't be.

Chapter Two

I'd lost sight of the man by the time I'd cleaned up after Angus and started back to the shop. He and I went back inside, and I went into the bathroom to wash my hands. The bell jingled, and I looked at my pale reflection in the mirror.

The man I'd seen was David. He was here. Or at least, someone who looked very like him—unbelievably like him—was running loose in Tallulah Falls.

I gulped, and then went out into the shop. I sighed with relief when I saw Vera Langhorne making herself comfy in one of the red club chairs.

"Hi!" she said. "I thought I'd stop by and stitch for a few minutes and talk with you about the masquerade ball."

The masquerade ball . . . right.

Vera was a little matronly, and she was currently dieting, exercising, and looking for a beau. In that state of mind, she wanted all her single, widowed, and divorced friends—me, included, natch—to live well and to look for love along with her. That attitude could get on your last nerve, but Vera was a wonderful alternative to finding David standing in my shop.

The latest attempt to "find us some men" was to take place at the masquerade ball next Saturday. The ball was billed as a Tallulah Falls Chamber of Commerce event to show its appreciation to all the local merchants, but in reality, anyone and everyone could come. I was having enough trouble choosing between Ted and Todd as it was without adding a huge event and expensive gown to the mix.

"Let's stitch." I sat on the sofa and picked up my Kuba cloth. It would do me good to work on the quilt and forget about wedding dresses for a few minutes.

Vera took up her latest project—quilt squares she was doing in redwork to match some pillowcases she'd made for her Victorian bedroom. "So, are you going to the ball?"

I inclined my head. "Probably not."

"I knew you'd need some convincing," she said, looking down at her belle-at-the-ball gown with fan and following the lines of the pattern with the red embroidery thread. "Why don't you want to go?"

"It's not that I don't want to go," I said, although that wasn't entirely true. "I just don't have anything to wear."

"That's ridiculous. Finding something to wear is half the fun of going to a ball in the first place!" She grinned. "And I just happened to see the most fabulous dress and mask in a little shop just outside Lincoln City. It's maroon and black, and it would look magnificent on you."

I wavered. A maroon and black ball gown with a matching feathered mask? How cool was that? "Was it very expensive?"

"Not very."

I bit my lip. The other reason I didn't want to go to the ball was that I was afraid that going with either Ted or Todd would mean I was with Ted or Todd, and I wasn't ready to form a steady relationship with either of them. At least, not yet. Particularly because I didn't know which one I wanted. If either. And I wasn't a hundred percent sure which one of them wanted me. If either! So there you go.

Besides that, Vera was loaded. Not very expensive to her could translate into very expensive for me.

"Come on," Vera prodded. "How often in your lifetime do you get a chance to attend a masquerade ball? I'm close to sixty, and this will be my first. It'll be great."

Close to sixty? Come on, Vera, I thought. "I'll think about it," I said.

"Promise?"

I smiled. "I promise."

Before resuming work on my Kuba cloth, I glanced out the window. I have to admit I was still halfway looking for the man who'd borne such a striking resemblance to David. This time, though, instead of David, I saw Ted. And he was yakking it up with some woman. A really pretty woman, to be exact, who'd thrown back her head and was laughing ever so merrily at something he'd said. They'd come from MacKenzies' Mochas and were both holding travel cups.

I didn't realize I was sitting there staring at the pair with my mouth hanging open until Vera spoke.

"Oh, Marcy, dear, don't trouble yourself about her. She's just some detective Ted has to train."

"Yeah," I said. "He looks really bothered by this burden that's been thrust upon him."

"She is striking, isn't she?"

"Yes, she is." She was everything I wasn't: tall, brunette, with an athletic build . . . and she had a position of authority. Some guys like that.

"I suppose I'd be jealous, too, if I were in your shoes," Vera said.

"I'm not jealous. I'm surprised, that's all." I tried to examine my feelings. I wasn't really jealous. Was I? I mean, we weren't in high school. I wasn't wearing Ted's class ring or his letter jacket and telling everyone we were going steady. Even if he was dating the "striking" detective, it wouldn't be any of my business. After all, he and I had been on a couple dates, had shared one kiss. And he knew I'd also been seeing Todd.

"Again, I wouldn't worry," Vera said. "From what I hear, he'll be training her for a few weeks and then she'll go off to a new unit or something or other."

"Right." I pointedly resumed stitching on the Kuba cloth.

"Besides," Vera said, absolutely refusing to let it go, "if Ted develops an interest in the lady detective, you've still got Todd on the string."

I did not have anyone on a string, and I didn't want to discuss my romantic life with Vera any more today. "The most interesting thing happened this morning," I said in order to change the subject. "I was passing by Nellie Davis's shop and saw someone who looked like a guy I used to know in San Francisco. Isn't that odd?"

She lifted and dropped her shoulders. "I dunno. They say everybody has a twin somewhere in the world. Do you believe that?"

"After this morning, I'm thinking that just might be possible."

After Vera left, I went back into the office to work on the third design for the wedding dress. I was still staring at the photograph and wondering what else I could do when the shop bell jingled and my best friend, Sadie, called out, "Marce, where are you?"

"I'm in the office. Come on back."

Sadie, also a tall brunette with an athletic build, sat on the chair beside my desk and peered over at my computer screen. "Is there something you've been neglecting to tell me?"

"*Ha-ha*. Do you know a Cassandra Wainwright?"

"*Um*, yes, I do," Sadie said. "It's rumored that she once died and went to hell, but the devil brought her back because she was too darn mean."

I chuckled. "That's encouraging. She's commissioned me to embellish her mother's vintage wedding gown for her wedding on—ready for this?—St. Valentine's Day."

"Cancel. Tell her you can't do it," Sadie said. "I'm telling you, the woman is bad news."

"Maybe you're right. All this looking at wedding dresses has me reliving a very painful part of my past. I even thought I saw David this morning as I passed by the aromatherapy shop."

"Oh, Marce, I'm sorry." Sadie blinked back sudden tears. "Call Cassandra Wainwright and tell her to forget it. Don't put yourself through this."

Sadie had been the matron of honor at my wedding. She and Blake had been happily married for five years. Lucky them.

A lump formed in my throat. "I thought I was

completely over him, Sadie. I thought all those feelings were behind me. But then she came in this morning and brought the dress . . . and I started thinking about my dress and how gorgeous it was and how Mom had worked so hard on it and then . . ."

Sadie hugged me, and we both shed a few tears.

"What a jerk," she said after a couple minutes. "He didn't even have the guts to confront you face-to-face."

"I think that's part of the reason it was so hard to let go," I said. "There was never any closure. I mean, there we were one evening, laughing and talking about our future . . . and then the next day he just didn't show up. He didn't call. He didn't send an e-mail . . . nothing. And then Tony came and basically told me good-bye from David."

She sighed. "I know. Blake and I drove around looking for David. It's probably good we didn't find him. Blake might not have been able to hold me off him."

I laughed as I took a tissue and then handed the box to Sadie. "I don't think he could have. You were so mad! But you looked beautiful. You have to admit, Mom didn't design tasteless bridesmaid dresses."

"No, indeed she did not," Sadie said, drying her eyes with the tissue. "Black taffeta with a white satin sash. I've worn that gown to a couple black-tie affairs since . . . you know, since then."

"I don't blame you. It's a classy dress."

"It is. And Beverly will come up with something even better for the next wedding."

"If there ever is a next wedding," I said glumly.

"Come on. Let's get you out of this funk. Are you going to the masquerade ball?"

"I don't know. Vera was in here talking about it earlier. She even said she saw a maroon and black gown and mask in a store outside Lincoln City that she felt would be perfect for me."

"*Ooh*, that does sound pretty," Sadie said. "My gown is royal blue."

"So you and Blake are going, then?"

"*Uh-huh*. We're catering, but since the Chamber of Commerce is generous and really because they want all the local business owners enjoying themselves at the party, they've included enough money for us to hire a wait staff and leave all of our staff in place at the shop. So we can oversee but still enjoy the ball."

I smiled. "That's great."

"Hasn't Todd spoken with you about it yet?"

"Not yet."

"He will," she said. "He's just been busy."

I nodded. "I saw Ted Nash and his new partner leaving your shop this morning. Did you get a chance to meet her?"

"Yeah. She seemed okay. A little reserved, though, if you ask me." She looked at my face.

"Does that bother you? That she's Ted's new partner, I mean."

"No. After this morning and my sudden hallucinations of David, I'm thinking I'm really not ready to even date anyone," I said. "Friends are enough for me right now. They don't rip out your heart and grind it into hamburger. That's why I don't know if I'll even go to this stupid masquerade ball."

"Come on. It'll be fun. And it's not an engagement party. Go with Todd. Dance, nosh, and kiss him at the midnight unmasking."

"We'll see." I jerked my head toward the shop. "Come on. Let's get out of here and stop looking at this depressing wedding gown."

"So, you're going to call and tell Cassandra you can't do the work?" Sadie asked as we stepped over Angus and walked to the sitting area.

"I don't know," I said, expelling a breath of frustration. "I mean, I can't let my past interfere with my present and my future, can I?"

Sadie pursed her lips but didn't say anything.

"I doubt she'll be happy with any of my designs, anyway," I said. "And you should've seen how she reacted to Angus. You'd have thought he was a two-headed dragon that went charging at her."

Sadie laughed and called Angus to her. He ambled over to sit at her feet. "I'd have given a hundred dollars—make that a hundred doggie treats—to have seen that," she told him as she scratched behind his ears. "Could you do it again when she comes back? Could you?"

He barked his consent.

"Good boy! You're a good boy! Yes, you are!" She noticed my face had frozen. "What's wrong?"

She followed my eyes to the door. My ex-fiancé, David Frist, was stepping through it.

"Hello, Marcy."

I couldn't find my voice. All I could do was stare. He looked pretty much the same—sandy blond hair falling over his forehead and into his green eyes à la Redford in *The Way We Were*, perfect smile, hands placed casually in his front jeans pockets. I noticed he was wearing a scarf I'd given him—it was green-and-white-striped, and it played up his eyes.

"Hi, David," I said.

"What are you doing here?" Sadie spat the words out as if they tasted as bitter as her voice sounded.

"Hello to you, too, Sadie," David said with a smile. "You're looking well." He nodded at Angus. "Nice dog."

"Thank you," I said. I felt paralyzed.

David gave me a bemused frown. "He's yours? I always thought if you ever had a dog, it would be a little long-haired lapdog."

Angus couldn't quite understand the underlying vibe in the room. He looked from me to Sadie and back again in confusion before realizing the tension was the newcomer's fault and uttering a low growl at David.

"Sadie, would you mind taking him for a quick walk?" I asked.

"I'll make it very quick," she said. She got up, hurried to the counter, and retrieved Angus' leash. "Come on, baby." She brushed by David, giving him a scathing look. "I'll be right back."

"Don't hurry back on my account," he said. He turned and watched Sadie march Angus down the street.

I noticed she went in the direction of MacKenzies' Mochas. She was going to tell Blake.

David turned back to me, took his hands from his pockets, and held out his arms. "Come here."

I hesitated.

"Just a hug," he said. "Please."

I slowly rose from the sofa and went to stand in front of him. At five feet tall, I barely reached his chest.

He enfolded me in his arms and lowered his face to the top of my head. "I've missed you so much."

Part of me wanted to yell at him, to scream and cry and tell him to get out of my shop. But somehow I allowed my arms to encircle his waist. He felt so familiar. I used to love for David to hold me. He'd made me feel so protected . . . secure . . .

loved. I closed my eyes. I couldn't do this to myself. I couldn't let this man come in here and hurt me all over again. I'd thought I was completely over him. I *was* completely over him. I took a firm step backward. But I couldn't just kick him out. This was a chance to get the answers I needed.

"Would you like to sit down?" I asked.

"Of course." He sat on the sofa Sadie had vacated, and I sat on one of the club chairs.

"What brings you to Oregon?"

"You."

Chapter Three

Before David could elaborate, Sadie, Blake, and Angus burst back into the shop.

"What do you mean coming in here like nothing ever happened?" Blake said.

Standing there with his hands on his hips, Blake actually kind of resembled David. They had the same hair color and fair complexion, but Blake was a little shorter and stockier than David.

"Blake, I don't want any trouble with you," David said.

"I know you don't," Blake said.

Blake had assumed the role of my big brother while he and Sadie were dating and Sadie was my roommate in college. "It's all right," I told him.

"It's not all right," Blake said. "He humiliated you in front of three hundred guests and then shows up today like he simply missed a dental appointment? I don't think so."

Angus growled.

"Sadie, please take Angus into the bathroom," I said.

Sadie did as I asked.

"I'd just like to talk with Marcy privately," David said. "Is that too much to ask?"

"No," I said. "It isn't."

Blake blew out an angry breath and shook his head. "Fine. But if you need me, you call me," he said to me. Then he turned to David. "And if . . . when Marcy tells you to leave, you'd better go."

Blake and Sadie left, but they peered in the window all the way down the sidewalk until they were out of sight.

I smiled nervously. "They mean well."

"I know they do. They love you," he said. "So do I."

Oh no, he didn't! He did not just say that! My mouth was dry, my hands were shaking, and I felt kind of queasy. "What are you doing here, David?"

"I've been doing a lot of soul searching the past few months." He leaned toward me, placing his forearms on his thighs. "I was dating this girl, but I got so bored with her I finally couldn't stomach even looking at her anymore. Not long after dumping her, I wound up losing my job. And you know what?"

I didn't answer, but he didn't really wait for a response, either.

"It didn't even matter. I realized my job wasn't that important to me. Nothing in my life meant much to me," he said. "That's a sad situation to find yourself in."

"I guess it is."

"So I started thinking back to the time when I was the happiest I'd ever been. It's the time I was with you." He reached out and took my hand. "Let's start all over."

I shook my head and fought to hold back tears. "There's too much water under that bridge to ever go there again. I could never trust you."

"Why not?" he asked. "I never cheated on you. I never lied to you."

"The last thing you told me before our wedding day was a lie. You said, 'See you tomorrow.'" I snatched my hand back away from him.

"I meant to be there," David said. "When I left your house that evening, it was my heartfelt intention to go through with the wedding. But the more I thought about it, the scarier that scenario seemed to me."

"How flattering. Thank you."

He stood and began pacing. "It wasn't you, Marcy. It was the responsibility. I wasn't ready to stand up and say, 'This is what I want to do with the rest of my life.' I didn't want to be responsible for a wife . . . for a family."

"And you couldn't have come to that conclusion—I don't know—a week before the wedding?" I asked, getting to my feet. "How about even a day before the wedding? You had to wait until the exact hour of the wedding to receive this revelation?" I stepped out of my heels and stood up on the ottoman so I could look David in the eye. "Do you know how hard my mother worked on that bridal gown?"

"Yes, I do." He strode to the front of the ottoman. "I hope you kept it."

The bells over the shop door jingled, causing both David and me to turn toward the sound. Todd walked through the door.

"Marcy, are you okay?" he asked. He walked by David, and held his hand out for me to hold on to as I stepped down from the ottoman. "It's all right. I'm here. Where did you see it?"

"See what?" I asked.

"The rat." Todd glanced around the shop, keeping one arm around my waist. "Sadie called and said you'd seen a huge rat. Where'd you see it last?"

"You just walked past it," I said wryly.

As Todd looked at the floor, David stepped forward and held out his hand. "David Frist, huge rat. Nice to meet you."

Todd shook David's hand. "Todd Calloway, huge rat removal service. Nice to meet you, too . . . I think." He gave me a wary look.

"Sadie is just playing a trick on all of us," I said with a forced laugh. "David is an old . . . friend . . . from San Francisco."

"An old friend, *huh*?" David gave me a rueful smile. "Oh well. I guess you could've said an old enemy."

"I need to get back to the Brew Crew," Todd said, as a couple young women came into the shop. "Let me know if you need anything."

"I will." I kissed his cheek. "Thank you for coming."

He nodded. "I'll check on you later."

I slipped my heels back on and went to attend to my customers. They were interested in latch-hooking. As David sat back down on the sofa, I took the women around to the latch-hook pillow and rug kits I had on hand and told them that if they didn't see anything that appealed to them, I could order whatever kit they'd like. One chose a lighthouse rug kit, and the other opted for a pillow kit featuring a panda. I rang up their purchases, placed them in periwinkle bags with the Seven-Year Stitch logo, and invited the women to check out my available embroidery classes.

"There are fliers inside your bags telling about each class," I said. "Please let me know if you're interested in one."

They thanked me and assured me they would look the fliers over. I had hoped David might leave while I attended to them, but no such luck.

After they left, he got up off the sofa and came over to the counter. "Is there something going on between you and the rat slayer?"

I shrugged. "We're friends."

"He appeared a little proprietary to me."

"That shouldn't matter to you anymore," I said.

"Maybe it shouldn't. But it does." He took both my hands. "I want you to think about the good times we've had, Marce. And I want you to think about the good times we can still have. It's up to you. It's not too late for us . . . not if you don't want it to be. Give me another chance."

I started to speak, but he interrupted me. "Don't say anything today. I'll stop back by and see you tomorrow."

"But—"

"Tomorrow," he repeated. And then he left.

At around five p.m., I locked up the shop and took Angus home for dinner. I had a class that night, so I planned to leave Angus in the fenced backyard while I went back to the shop. As Angus ate his food, I made myself a tuna salad sandwich. I took a can of Diet Coke from the fridge and sat down at the kitchen table to eat.

I got out my cell phone, put it on speaker, and called Mom.

"Beverly Singer," Mom trilled on the phone's third ring.

"Hi." I popped the top on the Diet Coke.

"You sound as if you're a million miles away," she said. "Where are you calling from?"

"The kitchen. But I have the phone on speaker. I'm eating my dinner."

"Oh, that's it, then." She paused. "Is everything all right?"

"No." I took a drink of my soda to relieve my dry mouth. "David came to see me today."

"David who?"

"Mom, you know David who," I said. "David Frist."

"I figured as much, but I was hoping maybe it was another David. David Boreanaz, maybe. David Ortiz. David Copperfield. I'd have even preferred David Lee Roth over David Frist," Mom said. "Has it really taken him this long to come crawling back to you?"

"You aren't surprised that he asked me to get back together with him?" I asked.

"Of course not. You were the best thing to ever happen to him. I'd heard he'd lost his job and his latest girlfriend. I didn't know he'd headed your way, though, or else I'd have warned you."

"You want to know an amazing coincidence?" I asked. "I was thinking about him just this morning." I explained to Mom about Cassandra Wainwright bringing her wedding dress in for embellishment and how it reminded me of the breathtaking gown she'd made me. "So, with all those memories flooding my mind, in walks David."

"You sound wistful, love."

"I'm wistful over what might have been, I guess," I said. "I was so full of hopes and expectations then. And I still think David and I could have had the most beautiful children. But I'm not considering getting back with him."

"Are you sure?" Mom asked. "You sound awfully vulnerable."

"That seems to be the general consensus," I said with a laugh. I told Mom about Sadie being in the shop when David first walked in and how she brought Blake over to try to intimidate David. "Then she called and told Todd that I'd seen a huge rat in the shop. Poor Todd rushed over to help out but had no idea what was really going on."

"That was terribly rude of her," Mom said. "I know Sadie's heart was in the right place, but this is your life. No one can tell you how to live it." She sighed. "Granted, I don't trust David not to hurt you again. But you have to follow your own heart. I just want you to be happy. It's all I've ever wanted."

"Thanks, Mom. I love you."

"I love you, too," she said. "And you'll have beautiful children no matter who you marry."

"Even David Lee Roth?" I asked with a giggle.

"Even him. But. Do. Not. Go. There."

I laughed. "Gotta run. I have to get back to the shop before class."

"Tell everyone hello for me."

Mom had charmed my friends and students when she came to visit. I promised I'd give her regards to Tallulah Falls. She was headed back to New York to a movie set the day after tomorrow, and she promised she'd give my regards to Broadway.

I ended the call and finished my sandwich and diet soda. Then I put my coat back on and let Angus into the backyard. Before locking up the house, I turned on a lamp in the living room as well as the outside lights. I wasn't paranoid, but I'd learned over the past five months that it paid to be careful. I hopped into my bright red Jeep and drove back to the shop.

As I drove, I couldn't avoid David's suggestion that I think about the good times we'd had together. If you try not to think about something, it's the only thing you can think about.

We'd first met when I delivered some financial documents to his employer. I'd been in the oh-so-exciting world of accounting then. Not to say I have anything against accounting. I mean, I'd gone to school and studied the subject for four years, and it had paid my bills for seven. But accounting wasn't what I'd been meant to do with my life.

Anyway, I'd taken the papers into David's offices on my way home from work. My boss had instructed me to have the company CEO sign the documents so I could take them back to the office the next morning. Naturally, the CEO had already left for the day.

I was more than a little ticked because the guy had known I was coming and had still left. I don't know if he'd simply forgotten about our appointment or if I hadn't been important enough for him to bother with. I asked the receptionist to call him at home to see if I could take the papers there for his signature. The last possible filing date was the next day, and I didn't want to get in trouble with my boss by failing to get this guy to sign the papers so I could send them in.

Instead, the panicky receptionist had called David. David was the human resources manager. He'd given me that million-dollar smile of his and had promised to take care of everything the next morning. Suddenly I wasn't so ticked anymore.

David had been true to his word. Or, at least, he had been on that occasion. He'd had the papers signed and had delivered them to my office just before noon. And then he'd taken me to lunch at a charming little bistro I'd never even heard of before. And I thought I'd been to every bistro in San Francisco!

The next day, David had taken me to dinner. After that, it seemed we couldn't get enough of each other. When we weren't together, we were on the phone talking to each other. I felt like a giddy teenager with her first crush.

David and me riding the Ferris wheel at the carnival. Laughing and holding hands as we walked in the rain with David holding his coat open, trying to shield me with it. Talking over coffee in the café around the corner from my apartment building until all hours. Opening the door first thing in the morning and finding a single red rose David had left for me.

I sniffled, tears streaming down my cheeks. Chords of "The Way We Were" played in my head.

Maybe the song was right in that people suppress memories that are too painful to remember. In addition to that one biggie I simply couldn't forget—being left at the altar—I tried to dredge up some of those bad memories of David to counter the good ones.

That's how I'd gotten through the breakup originally. I'd thought of all the reasons why David had done the best thing for the both of us. Now I needed to bring those reasons back to the forefront of my mind and remind him—and myself—of them . . . remind us both why we weren't good for each other, after all.

I remembered the times David had accused me of being too dependent on my mother. He wasn't very close to his own parents, and he resented my relationship with her. He thought I gave her too much say in my life, that I spoke to her over the phone and visited her too often, and that I talked about her too much to his friends. He'd said I was constantly bragging about her being a hotshot in the movie business and was trying to impress everyone. In truth, I couldn't remember speaking to any of them about her except once when one of them asked me if my mom was Beverly Singer, the costume designer. I couldn't have cared less what his friends thought of me or my mother. I only wanted David to be proud of me and happy with me.

And I remembered how snobbishly he'd behaved toward Sadie and Blake. He'd acted as if they were flower children or something because they owned a coffee shop on the Oregon coast.

"Do they think MacKenzies' Mochas will be the next Starbucks or something?" he'd asked.

"They're not trying to be the next Starbucks," I'd tried to explain. "They're doing what they love. I think it's wonderful."

"Wonderful? Maybe. Practical? Hardly."

Oh yeah, David could be condescending, rude, crass, and arrogant. I parked the Jeep in front of the Seven-Year Stitch, turned off the engine, and dug in the glove box for a tissue. I wiped my eyes and then took my makeup kit out of my purse and touched up my makeup. I didn't want my class to arrive and see that I'd been crying.

I put the kit back into my purse and got out of the Jeep. As soon as I walked up the two steps to the sidewalk, I saw it. A single red rose in a vase by the front door.

It was a good thing I still had my makeup kit.

"Marcy!"

I fought back the tears and turned to see Todd jogging across the street toward me.

"Hi!" I called, unlocking the door and picking up the vase. "Come on in." I flipped the lights on and set the vase on the counter. "Let me put my coat and purse in the office, and I'll be right back. Want me to hang up your jacket?"

"No," he said. "I'm fine. Thanks."

I returned to find him sitting on the sofa facing the window. His black leather jacket was draped over one of the chairs. I sat down beside him.

"I'm sorry about what Sadie did to you today," I said. "Having you rush over here for nothing wasn't funny."

He shrugged. "She sounded really upset over the phone, and she said you were freaking out."

"Well, I was. But she should've told you the truth. Remember—"

"She told me," Todd interrupted. "I called her when I got back to the Brew Crew, and she explained the whole thing. Are you all right?"

"I'm fine. It was just a shock to see David. I hadn't even spoken with him since the night before we were supposed to have been married."

"I'm sorry."

Todd seemed ill at ease—like he didn't know

what to do or how to act. Maybe he thought I'd decided to get back with David. I wanted to let him know I had no intention of doing that, without coming right out and saying so.

"Thank you again for coming by and checking on me."

"You're welcome," he said, smiling slightly. "I just wanted you to know I'm here for you . . . and that you can count on me."

Class did me good that evening. Vera was there, along with Julie Clark and her daughter, Amber (both of whom have been taking classes since I first came in October), two of Amber's friends from school—Carlie and Jennica (all three pretty, outgoing teens), and a couple of newcomers. I asked the new students to introduce themselves to the class.

Both were older women, and they looked at each other and then at everyone else shyly.

"I suppose I can go first," said one, who had tight white curls, blue eyes, and silver wire-rimmed glasses. "I'm Berta Ginsberg. Molly and I are from up the coast a little ways. We heard about your classes, and we thought we'd give this one a try. I hope you aren't too far along to be able to teach us something."

"Not at all, Berta," I said. "We're only in the second week of this candlewicking course. I think you'll pick it up very quickly." I smiled at the other woman, whose hair was as brown and straight as Berta's was white and curly. "Molly, is it?"

Molly nodded. "Yep. Molly Simcox. Nice to meet everybody."

Molly was apparently a woman of few words. "Nice to meet you, Molly," I said. The other students murmured their assent.

I went to the counter and got the photos Reggie had sent. "Reggie sends her regards from India." I started passing the photos at each end of the square. "It looks like she and Manu are having a blast."

"It sure does," Vera said. "I've never been to India. I think I might like to go there sometime."

"Talk with Reggie when she gets back," Julie said. "Maybe she can help you make the arrangements."

"Maybe so." Vera smiled. "I will be glad for them to get home, though."

"Me, too," I said. "I miss them."

"Not only that," Vera said. "Something bad always happens when the sheriff is out of town.'

Chapter Four

Unfortunately, I'd been unable to come up with a third design idea for the wedding gown that I thought might satisfy Cassandra Wainwright. But, on the other hand, I wasn't sure I intended to take on the project, anyway. If Cassandra didn't like either of the two designs I presented her with, maybe she'd take her project elsewhere and I would at least know I had tried. It would be horrible of me to have told her yesterday that I'd be happy to do the work and then cop out on her today because my battered ego made it too hard for me to work on a wedding dress.

If Cassandra backed out of the project, then fine. If not, I would do the work.

Since Cassandra and her fiancé were to be coming in today, I'd left Angus at home playing in the backyard this morning. I'd only been at the shop for an hour and was busy replenishing my supply of perle flosses when Cassandra, her fiancé, and an older woman came in. I was thinking the woman had to be Cassandra's future mother-in-law, given her resemblance to the fiancé. Both the fiancé and his mother had black hair—though it was rather obvious the mom was helping hers stay black at this point—olive complexions, and dark brown eyes. Cassandra's fiancé was wearing khaki slacks, a cream-colored sweater, and a brown tweed sport coat. I couldn't tell what the older woman was wearing beneath her black wool coat, but Cassandra was resplendent in a red leather coat and dark denim jeans.

"Good morning," I said brightly. "May I take your coats?"

"No, thank you. Where's the dog?" Cassandra said, looking all around the shop.

"I left him at home today," I said.

"Oh, good." She held her open palm toward her fiancé. "This is my fiancé, Frederic Ortega, and his mother, Francesca."

"Hello," I said, shaking hands with both Frederic and his mother. "It's a pleasure to meet you both."

"Have you prepared your design ideas?" Cassandra asked, moving over to the seating area.

"I have, and I printed them out yesterday," I said as I went to retrieve the photos from the office. I returned to the seating area, where Cassandra and Frederic were sitting on the sofa facing the window, and Francesca was sitting on one of the red chairs.

"I only have two that I feel could be done in the time allotted and with the materials you mentioned." I handed the photos to a dubious-looking Cassandra.

She gave the first photo—Look One—a cursory glance before tossing it onto the ottoman in front of Francesca. Look Two—the one with the triangular jeweled insets topped with sapphires on the skirt and the jeweled bodice—received a grudging respect.

"This one has possibilities," Cassandra said, showing the photo to Frederic. "Don't you think?"

"It's lovely," he said. "Mom, what do you think?"

Francesca leaned over to look at the photo in Cassandra's hand. "I like it."

"It could work," Cassandra said. "I really like how you've done the skirt on this one. I'm not so crazy about the big blue jewel at the top of the bodice, but we can work on that. For now, let's start with you doing the skirt just as you have it in this photo."

"All right," I said.

Francesca opened her enormous black purse and removed a blue velvet bag. "Here are the gems we'd like you to put on the dress." She handed me the bag.

"May I?" I asked before opening the bag.

At Francesca's nod, I opened the bag and carefully poured the gems onto the oval coffee table that sat between the two sofas. If I hadn't known these were fake, I could certainly mistake them for the real things.

"These are beautiful," I said.

"Thank you," Francesca said. "I'm unable to give much of a gift to my son and his bride on their wedding day, but this I can do."

"I think it's a wonderful gesture," I said. "And these gems will give the dress such an opulent look."

"They will, won't they?" Cassandra said, her eyes gleaming. She opened her own bag—a red leather clutch that matched her coat—and took out a checkbook. "Do you intend to work by the hour or by the piece?"

"I typically work by the piece," I said. "But I can work by the hour if that would be better for you. It's whatever you want to do."

"You can work by the hour, then," she said. "That way, I won't feel guilty if I have to have you do something over and over until you get it right." She smiled, but there really wasn't a lot of humor there. "I'll give you a five-hundred-dollar retainer today, and after you've finished the skirt, we'll see where you're at."

"Five hundred?" Frederic said.

"You don't think it's enough?" Cassandra asked.

"I . . . I suppose it's all right," he said.

I had a feeling he'd been going to object to her giving me a retainer—or, at least, that much of one—but after the "over and over" comment, I kind of felt like I'd need it. I gladly accepted the check and wrote Cassandra a receipt.

"I'll be in tomorrow or the next day to see how you're doing," Cassandra said.

"Great," I said. "I appreciate your business. Francesca, Frederic, it was a pleasure meeting the two of you."

"You as well," Francesca said.

Frederic merely nodded and left.

Once they were out on the street, I could see him engage Cassandra in a rather heated debate. It didn't last long, though, and it was easy to see that he was letting her have her way on whatever they'd been arguing about—my retainer, I imagined.

I sat down on the sofa facing the window and reopened the blue velvet bag. I examined each of the gems prior to putting them back into the bag. I wanted to make sure I had enough to make the skirt look as pretty as it did in the photograph. It appeared there were plenty of crystals. Like Cassandra had said, they appeared to be about a third of a carat each. The saltwater pearls varied in size from five millimeters all the way up to nine. There were at least ten of the sapphire-colored gems Cassandra had spoken of. They were dark blue, multifaceted jewels. I'd expected the blue gems to be round like the pearls and crystals. Instead, they were emerald cut. They were beautiful. At first glance, no one would be able to tell these jewels were costume jewelry if they were set in a ring or pendant.

I made a mental note to ask Francesca where she got them. I'd never seen imitation jewels of this quality before, and I'd love to have some. I'd even like to carry them in the store. Not only would they be great for embroidery projects, but they'd be fantastic for costumes. If I decided to go to the masquerade ball, I'd love to use beads and paste gems like these to make myself some "ruby" jewelry to go with that maroon and black gown Vera had told me about.

I took the velvet bag and the wedding gown into the office. I then went into the stockroom and got a dress form. I carried the dress form into the office and slipped the wedding dress onto it. I then put the dress form on a wooden stool so I could use straight pins to measure out where the triangular insets would be placed on the dress. Using my tape measure, I made each of the insets four inches long at the base and three inches apart. That would adequately cover all the yellowing along the skirt's hem without overwhelming the gown. We wanted opulence, not a blinding Vegas-showgirl wedding gown.

I'd pinned the dress all the way around the

hem when the bells over the shop door indicated I had a customer.

"Good morning!" I called. I got up off the floor, slid my palms down the sides of my jeans, and set my pin cushion on the desk before going out into the store.

"Good morning."

It wasn't a customer. It was David. Well, I suppose he could buy something, which would make him a customer, but I doubted he would. I mean, one, he was out of work and, two, he didn't embroider . . . as far as I knew.

Okay, so my mind rambles when I'm not prepared for something. You'd think that after yesterday, I'd have been prepared to see David today. But I'd pretty much put yesterday's visit and the things David had said in a little lead-lined box and stored it in a dark corner of my mind to be ignored until I was ready to deal with it. And I wasn't ready to deal with it yet.

"Hi," I said, wary.

David nodded toward the rose adorning my countertop. "I see you found it."

"Yeah. Thanks."

"You're welcome." He walked slowly toward me. "I've missed you so much."

I nodded. Had I missed him? Sure. But for a long time—months, I suppose—all I had felt for David and our relationship had been anger and regret. I finally was able to look back on the good times we'd had and smile, but getting to that point had been hard. It was still hard.

"I just can't get past what you did to me, David."

"I said I'm sorry," he said. "What do I have to do?"

"You don't have to do anything." I walked over to the seating area and sat on one of the chairs. "I didn't ask you to come here. I've moved on with my life."

"Marcy, we were great together. We could have a terrific future . . . starting now. I've matured. I'm ready to settle down, buy the house with the picket fence, have a family."

I looked down at my hands. I'd once wanted nothing more than to make a life with this man. Was it possible for us to pick up the pieces? After the way he'd hurt me, would I even want us to?

David sat on the sofa beside my chair and took my hands in his. "I know this whole thing comes as a surprise to you."

"A surprise? That's the understatement of the year."

"But I'm willing to give you time," he said. "I'll be here for at least a week."

"An entire week. That is a lot of time."

"Be as sarcastic as you want, but I'm going to be here every day of that week convincing you that giving me another chance—giving us another chance—is the right thing to do." He raised my hand to his lips and kissed it. "Have dinner with me tonight. You'll see. It'll be just like old times."

I pulled my hand away. "I can't tonight," I said. "I left Angus at home today, and I'll have to run home and feed him and then hurry back here for class."

"I can't do this by myself, Marcy." He blew out a breath. "Do you want to look back at your life ten years from now and wonder what might've been if you'd met me halfway?"

Did I? Maybe I should go out to dinner with him, see if there were any of those old feelings left. If nothing else, it would bring me the closure I hadn't had before.

I sighed. "Can we have dinner tomorrow evening? We can do it either before class or after."

"Do you have class every freakin' night?" he asked.

"I have class Tuesdays, Wednesdays, and Thursdays. If you'll recall, I had no idea you were coming. You can't expect me to rearrange my schedule at the last minute."

"Let's just have dinner Friday, then. Can you do that?"

"Yes, I can."

"Great," he said, standing. "I'll see you then." He stalked out the door.

I was glad for his semitantrum. It was a good reminder of the side of David I'd glossed over when we were dating.

He walked in the direction of MacKenzies' Mochas. I didn't think he'd go into the coffee shop, given his feelings about Blake and Sadie—and vice versa—but I guessed he'd had to park near there. And I also guessed Sadie would catch a glimpse of him walking past her window and would be over here as soon as she could.

I was a good guesser.

Sadie hadn't even stopped to grab a coat before rushing out of the shop and up the street to the Seven-Year Stitch. "What is up with him?" she asked as soon as she opened the door.

"He wants me. He needs me. He loves me. He can't live without me," I said.

"And it took him over a year to come to these conclusions?" she asked, coming over and flopping onto the sofa.

"It was mean of you to call Todd to come over here yesterday to chase away the big rat," I said.

"Yeah, well . . . ," she huffed. "I wanted to remind you that David isn't your only option. Todd's ten times better looking than David. And he's a good guy. If he made a promise to you, he'd keep it."

"I know you meant well, but it made all of us very uncomfortable—Todd included."

"I know," she said. "He called and fussed at me, too. So, what's the deal? Are you considering getting back with David?"

"No," I said. "But I need to get some closure. We're having dinner together Friday night."

"That won't give you enough time," she said, pushing a strand of her long dark hair out of her face. "He'll act as perfect as he can, and you'll think he's come to his senses."

"I'll know, Sadie. Trust me."

"I do trust you," she said. "It's him I don't trust."

I laughed. "Do you know how many fathers of teenage girls just uttered that exact same phrase? It's probably echoing somewhere in outer space in every language in the universe."

"Just guard your heart, Marce. I don't want to see you hurt again."

"That makes two of us."

When the alarm went off the next morning, it seemed as loud as a foghorn. Which was appropriate, I supposed, because I felt like I was in a fog. I reached over and slapped the clock. Snooze. Ten more minutes. Just ten. . . .

Suddenly a bell rang. It was loud. Grandfather-clock-in-my-head loud. I slapped the clock again, but the bell still rang. As I tried to shake off the fog and open my eyes to determine the source of the noise, it rang a third time.

I finally pried my eyes open and realized that it was the phone. I grabbed it. "What?" Okay. So it wasn't my usual chipper greeting, but I really hadn't slept well the night before and someone was calling me before I was even awake and I was foul over it.

"Marcy, this is Ted Nash."

"Oh, good grief. Did Sadie ask you to call me?"

"No. I . . . I'm afraid I need you to come on down to the shop," he said.

"Why?" I asked.

"There's been an accident."

My alarm went off for the second time. I fumbled around and turned it off.

"What kind of accident?" I asked. "A fire?" I shot up in bed. "Did my shop catch on fire?"

"No, it wasn't a fire. The shop is fine. However, there was a woman stabbed outside the store this morning. We found your name and number written on a piece of paper in her coat pocket. Get here as soon as you can, all right?" And then he hung up.

Now I was wide awake, but dread was holding me to the bed, urging me to get back under the covers and hide. I fought the dread—mainly because I didn't want Ted to come and drag me out of my house in my pj's—and got up. I quickly dressed and brushed my teeth. This could not be happening to me again. Could it?

I let Angus out into the backyard. I put his food and water out there with him, and I left. I wanted to take Angus with me so badly, especially since I'd left him home yesterday. But, if the Seven-Year Stitch was once again a crime scene, it was the last place he needed to be.

My heart had been racing as I drove to the shop, but when I got close enough to see the police cars and the ambulance, I thought it would stop beating entirely. I pulled closer and was stopped by a tall, uniformed police officer with blond hair and piercing green eyes.

"This is a crime scene," said the young officer, whose nameplate read *Moore*. "You can't go any farther."

"It's okay, Andrew," Ted called, approaching us. "This is Marcy Singer. It's her shop. Let her through."

Ted's deep blue eyes searched my face as he gave me instructions on where to park. I wanted to tell him I was all right, but I wasn't entirely sure if I was or not. When I got out of the Jeep, he accompanied me to the sidewalk where a portion had been cordoned off with yellow police tape. In my sneakers, I only reached Ted's chest. Part of me wanted to hide my face in his gray oxford shirt, but I knew I had to look.

Crime scene technicians were bending over the body. I couldn't see much . . . just her shoes. They were black, thick-heeled pumps. One shoe had been knocked off.

Keeping a hand at my lower back, Ted instructed the technicians to back away so I could view the body. I was glad of his support. Maybe if I fainted, he'd either catch me or at least keep me from cracking my head open on the concrete.

When the techs moved away, I gasped. "Francesca!"

"So you do know the victim?" Ted asked.

I nodded. "Francesca Ortega. She's Cassandra Wainwright's future mother-in-law."

"Not anymore, she isn't."

I turned to see who the woman with the abrasive voice—and attitude—was. It was the pretty woman I'd seen Ted with on Tuesday. I ignored her and looked back at Ted. "What happened?"

"She was stabbed here early this morning," he said.

"Was it a robbery?" I asked.

"We're not positive yet, but we think so. The victim didn't have a purse on her when we arrived." He nodded, and the crime scene investigators returned to their duties. "You're shivering. Let's go inside."

We moved around the body, and I unlocked the door. "This is such a shock. We need to contact Frederic, her son." I went to the counter where I had Cassandra's contact information. I gave it to Ted.

He led me over to the seating area, where we both sat on the navy sofa facing the window. He took a small, clear plastic bag from his jacket pocket. It contained a blue velvet drawstring bag. "We found this near the body. It's empty."

My eyes widened. The drawstring bag was just like the one in which Francesca had brought the gems I was going to use to adorn the dress. "She must've been afraid I wouldn't have enough and had brought more."

"More what?" Ted asked.

"More fake gems," I said. "Francesca brought some yesterday to be put on Cassandra's wedding gown. The robber must've thought they were real."

The abrasive woman entered the shop. "Where were you this morning, Ms. Singer?"

"I was in bed asleep," I said.

"Can anyone verify that?" she asked.

"Just Angus."

I saw Ted's lips twitch.

"Then can you have him come down here and give us his statement?" she demanded.

"No," I said. "He's a dog."

"Then you'd better not leave town." After glaring at me, the detective turned and went back outside.

"What's her problem?" I asked Ted.

"She's a rookie."

"Is she right?" I asked. "Am I a suspect?"

He sighed. "At this point, I'm afraid everyone's a suspect."

Chapter Five

"Tell me what you know about Francesca Ortega," Ted said.

"Only that her son is engaged to Cassandra Wainwright and that Francesca gave the bride and groom some gems to embellish a vintage wedding gown I'm customizing for Cassandra," I said. "I think Cassandra said the dress had belonged to her mother. Since you found that bag on the street, I guess maybe Francesca had more she wanted to include." I closed my eyes and sank back into the sofa cushions.

"I'd like to hug you right now," he said quietly, "but that wouldn't be wise."

"I know. The rookie wouldn't like it." I sighed. "And, once again, I'm back in the middle of a mess."

"It's not that bad," he said. "Maybe one of your

neighbors will be able to verify that your Jeep was at home this morning."

"Maybe." I began thinking about Mom . . . and San Francisco . . . and David. Maybe I should give David another chance. Maybe I should go back home. Maybe Tallulah Falls wasn't the place for me after all.

"Everything will be okay," Ted said. "It always has been so far, right?"

"So far," I said. "Why does this keep happening to me? Is Tallulah Falls trying to tell me something? Like 'go away'?" This was the third "accident"—okay, the first two were murders and this obviously was, too—to occur in or near my shop since I arrived a few months ago.

"It's a coincidence." He gave my hand a quick squeeze. "I need to get back out there. Will you be all right?"

I nodded.

Before Ted could leave, David came rushing into the shop, followed closely by the rookie, whose name I didn't even know yet. David's face was ashen. Rookie's face was grim.

"Marcy, are you all right?" David rushed over and gathered me into his arms.

"I'm fine," I said.

"When I saw all those police cars and the ambulance outside your shop, I thought something terrible had happened to you." He pulled away slightly to look at my face. "You're sure you're okay?"

"Yes. The victim was the mother of— Well, I knew her," I said. "I think she was coming to see me."

"So you'd planned to meet her here?" Rookie asked.

"Of course not," I said. "If I'd planned to meet her, I'd have been here when she arrived."

David moved to sit beside me on the sofa. He placed his arm around me protectively. I was surprisingly okay with it under the circumstances.

"Marcy, this is Detective Harriet Sloan," Ted said. "Detective Sloan, this is Marcy Singer."

Detective Sloan afforded me a curt nod. "Why do you think she was coming to see you?"

"As I explained to Detective Nash," I said, "she'd brought some gems in a blue bag—like the one he found on the sidewalk—to me yesterday. She wanted me to put them on a dress I'm embellishing for her future daughter-in-law. I'm guessing she didn't know what time the shop opened but that she wanted to bring some additional gems in case I needed them for the dress."

"I've called Ms. Wainwright," Detective Sloan told Ted. "She and Mr. Ortega should be here soon."

Ted was looking curiously at David. "And, sir, you are?"

"David Frist," he answered.

"He said he's the shop owner's fiancé," Detective Sloan said.

"You didn't have to be so dramatic," Ted said. "If you're a friend of Mar—Ms. Singer's—we'd have let you inside."

"I'm more than a friend of Marcy's," David said. "We were engaged once. If I have my way about it, we will be again."

Ted's jaw tightened. "Where were you this morning between seven and eight o'clock?"

"My hotel," David said. He dug in his wallet and produced a receipt. "See? I was having breakfast."

Detective Sloan leaned over to peer at the receipt. "Pretty convenient. Having an alibi for the very time you'd need one."

David scowled at her. "I didn't know I'd be needing an alibi. If I had, I wouldn't have dined alone."

She lowered the corners of her mouth. "Good point. Still, don't leave town."

"I don't intend to," David said. He looked at me. "Not without Marcy, anyway."

I knew Ted was looking at me, too, but I avoided looking at anyone. I simply stared down at the floor. I felt like I was in an episode of a soap opera. I had more drama in my life right now than I could handle.

Or so I thought. Apparently, I was wrong. The rest of the cast was on cue to arrive.

Todd and Sadie came sprinting through the door one right after the other. Todd had been a gentleman and had let Sadie go first. Still, he reached the sofa before she did.

"Marcy!" Todd exclaimed, rushing to sit on my other side. He took my hand. "Sweetheart, are you all right?"

Sadie wedged herself between David and me, flinging his arm away. She took my other hand. "Tell us what happened."

"This is ridiculous," Detective Sloan said to me. "Are you queen of the Oregon coast or something?"

"What's it to you if she is?" Sadie asked sharply. "She's our friend. And when we saw all the commotion over here, we were worried about her." She turned back to me. "Say something, Marce."

I looked past them through the window to the street where I could see the crime scene technicians loading Francesca's body into the ambulance. "It's Francesca, the mother of Cassandra Wainwright's fiancé," I said. "Someone stabbed her and robbed her . . . right out there in front of my store this morning."

"In broad daylight?" Todd asked. "And no one saw anything?"

"Not a thing," Ted said. "No one reported any screaming. We had officers speak with people in the neighboring shops. No one heard or saw a thing . . . or, if they did, they're not opening up about it."

Sadie nodded. "Some officers talked with

Blake. I hadn't gotten in yet. No one in MacKenzies' heard a thing."

"How could she be attacked and not make a sound?" I asked.

"The attacker killed her so quickly, she didn't see what was coming," Detective Sloan said. "He knew what she had, and he—or she—wanted it."

"What?" I asked. "You mean the fake jewels?"

"We'll be taking what you have here and having them appraised as soon as the techs finish up," Detective Sloan said.

"You don't think they're fake?" I asked. "They were being put on a wedding gown, for goodness' sake. No one but an actual queen would put real jewels on a wedding gown!"

"Speaking of that wedding gown, we'll need to take that with us, too," Detective Sloan said. "Where is it?"

"It's in my office." I stood and made my way through the maze of people gathered around me.

Detective Sloan followed me to the office. I could hear the people in the shop talking in a hushed buzz of voices. It sounded like a muffled beehive.

The dress form still stood on the stool. I'd finished two of the inserts yesterday. With the police confiscating the gown, there would be no way I could possibly get the embellishments finished before Valentine's Day. I took the dress form off the stool and placed it on the floor. Then I unzipped the gown, removed it from the form, and handed it to Detective Sloan.

"I have a garment bag for it," I said. "Would you like to put it in that?"

"Yeah. That'll do for now," she said. "I'll need the gems as well."

I held the garment bag for Detective Sloan to lower the gown into. As she zipped the bag, I retrieved the gems.

"Thanks for your cooperation." She gave me that curt nod she was so adept at, and then she went back out into the shop.

I considered crawling under my desk and hiding, but instead, I ambled back into the shop.

"We have everything we need," Ted told me softly, pulling me aside. "I'll let you know what we find out as soon as I can."

"All right," I said.

"Why don't you just close up shop and go home today?" he whispered. "You look tired. Have you eaten?"

I smiled. "I'll be fine. Thank you."

His eyes cut to the sofa. "Yeah, I guess you don't need me to hover. You have enough people doing that."

"Don't," I said gently. "I'll explain everything later. It's not as nuts as it seems. Okay, right now it is, but . . ."

He smiled. "Officers Moore and Taylor will be outside for a while. They're waiting on Ortega.

They're to bring him to the morgue. Call me if you need me."

"I will. Thanks."

"Detective Sloan," he called. "Let's go."

I walked back to the sitting area where David, Sadie, and Todd were still ensconced on the sofa. They were all looking at me expectantly, and I didn't have any answers. I sank onto the red chair. Tears threatened, but I didn't dare let them fall. David, Todd, and Sadie would trip over themselves getting me a tissue. Don't get me wrong. It's wonderful to be cared about. But at that moment, it was a little suffocating.

"I'm going to run next door and get you a latte and a muffin," Sadie said. "Will you be all right while I'm gone?"

I nodded. "That would be terrific. Thank you."

"Is there anything else you need?" Todd asked. "Is Angus all right?"

"He's fine. I put his breakfast outside before I left. By now, he's probably napping on the porch swing."

Todd chuckled. "I'd like to see that. Want me to go get him for you?"

I smiled up at him, my eyes brimming with those unshed tears. "Would you?"

"Of course." He gave me a quick hug. "Be back in a few minutes."

As soon as the door closed behind Todd, David said, "Thank goodness those two got out of our way."

"Got out of our way?" I asked. "They're both going to do things for me. They weren't in my way."

"I know," he said. "That just came out wrong. Tell me what's going on here. What happened to that woman? Why are they saying we can't leave town until they're sure of what happened to her?"

"Because she was stabbed outside my store, and she and I have a connection," I said. "You heard me telling the detectives about the wedding gown and the fake gems."

"Yeah, only they don't think they're fake. And apparently whoever stabbed the old gal on the sidewalk didn't think they were, either."

My lips tightened. "Her name was Francesca. I barely knew her, but she wasn't an 'old gal.' She seemed to be a very nice person."

The door opened so quickly, the bells barely had time to jingle before Cassandra swept into the shop with Frederic following in her wake.

"Where's my mother?" he asked. He clearly didn't know she was dead. Poor man.

"The ambulance pulled away with her about ten minutes ago," David answered. "I'm really sorry, man."

"Two officers are waiting outside to take you . . . to her," I said.

Frederic looked at Cassandra. "Let's go."

"Wait," she said. "What about my dress?" She glanced at Frederic. "While we're here, I might as well ask." She turned back to me. "Have you gotten very far on it?"

"I got the first two of the insets done, but the police confiscated it," I said. "I don't see how I can possibly get it finished in time if they don't give it back today or tomorrow at the latest. I'll return your retainer."

Cassandra huffed. "I can't believe this! The accident didn't happen in here. It happened on the street! And what does it have to do with my wedding gown? Why would the police take it?" She barked out a screech and shook her head. "They are not getting away with this. I'm going down there right now to give those people a piece of my mind."

"I need to see my mother," Frederic said.

"And the police will know where she is," Cassandra said. "Marcy, I'll be back with that gown. Count on it."

"My mother is lying somewhere in a hospital, and all you can think about is a dress?" Frederic asked.

David and I shared a glance.

Cassandra rolled her eyes. "Of course I'm concerned about your mother. But she'll be fine. I only hope she can identify the jerk who did this to her." She strode to the door and then stood until Frederic opened it for her.

She stepped through the door, once again shaking out her mane of curls. Frederic stepped over to the area of the sidewalk blocked off by crime scene tape. There was some blood on the sidewalk, although not as much as one would think. It seemed more blood had pooled on top of the body than beneath it.

"Don't torture yourself!" Cassandra called to him.

I slowly joined David on the sofa as Cassandra went to Frederic, took his arm, and pulled him in the opposite direction. She was speaking to him, and he was nodding his head. Hopefully, she was telling him they had to get to his mother.

Officer Moore approached the couple and led them toward his patrol car.

"Frederic doesn't know," I said softly.

"No, he doesn't. They must've only told him that his mother had been mugged." David put his arm around me again. It felt so familiar that I just let myself lean into it. "I'm just glad you're okay. If you'd have come in early or something, that could've been you."

"Thanks for being here."

He kissed the top of my head. "I want to be here for you forever."

I closed my eyes, blocking out the image on the street . . . trying to block out the image of Frederic looking at the spot where his mother had lain. "Poor Frederic. Poor Francesca."

Sadie returned with a vanilla latte with a hint

of cinnamon and a pumpkin muffin. "Where's Todd?"

"He went to get Angus," I said.

"Oh, that was sweet of him," she said.

"Wasn't it?" I said, and gratefully accepted the latte and the muffin. "And this was sweet of you. Thank you." I went on to explain about Cassandra and Frederic coming in after she and Todd had left. "They think Francesca is in the hospital."

"You mean, they don't know?" Sadie asked.

I shook my head and bit into my muffin.

"That's awful," she said.

"And what's worse," David said, "is that the bride was way more interested in her gown than in her fiancé's mother."

I nodded. "She said she'd be back here with the gown today. She was outraged that the police had confiscated it."

"This whole thing is weird," Sadie said, settling back against the cushions of the navy sofa opposite David and me. "The attacker apparently knew what he was doing in order to kill that poor little woman with one blow, and he believed whatever she had was worth killing her in broad daylight for. And not just in broad daylight, but during a really busy time. Do you know how many people are in and out of the coffee shop between seven and eight o'clock in the morning?"

"I do," I said. "Well, not really, but I imagine

there are a bunch." I sipped my latte. "That was a really huge risk, wasn't it?"

"Enormously huge," Sadie said.

"Maybe it wasn't a robbery, then. Maybe it was something else." I shrugged. "Maybe there was some sort of hit out on Francesca." I frowned and shook my head. "That doesn't make any sense. Who could that sweet old lady hurt or make angry enough that they'd want to kill her?"

"Her daughter-in-law, maybe?" David spread his hands. "I'm just saying that woman is one I'd definitely want to steer clear of."

"As much as I hate to agree with you," Sadie said to David, "I agree with you. Cassandra Wainwright is bad news."

"Still," I said, "I don't think she'd put a contract out on her mother-in-law."

"No," Sadie said. "I believe that if Cassandra wanted to kill someone, she'd just do it herself."

I'd finally convinced both David and Sadie to go and let me get some work done. Todd had dropped off Angus but then had to go to work himself. He said he'd check on me later—the same thing David and Sadie had promised. I needed to call Mom sometime today and let her know about the latest misadventure surrounding the Seven-Year Stitch. And I knew she'd be curious to know what was going on between David and me.

It had been a busy morning in the shop. Many were my normal customers, but some newcomers came in to try to get inside information on Francesca Ortega.

Not having the dress to work on, I had resumed work on the Kuba cloth quilt. I was alone in the sit-and-stitch square when Ted and Detective Sloan returned to the shop. I set the quilt aside and stood to greet them. Or rather, I rose to greet Ted.

"Hi," I said to him. "Did you talk with Frederic and Cassandra?"

"We did," he said.

"They were here right after you guys left. Frederic didn't know about his mother."

Ted nodded. "He does now."

"I'm so sorry."

"Did you have those gems out where people shopping here could see them?" Detective Sloan asked.

"Of course not. I kept them in my office where I was working on the dress," I said. "When I'd hear someone come into the shop, I'd stop working and go out to see how I could help them."

"The jewels are real," Ted said. "And they have an estimated value of seventy-five thousand to a hundred thousand dollars."

Chapter Six

No sooner had Ted told me the estimated worth of the gems than Cassandra and Frederic came into the shop. Cassandra stormed in, but Frederic followed slowly behind her. Given his bleak eyes and drawn mouth, I guessed the pair had just come from identifying his mother.

"We went back to the station after going to the morgue, but they told us you were here," Cassandra said to Ted and Detective Sloan. "Have you caught the guy who did this yet?"

"Not yet," Ted said.

"Why not?" she asked.

"Frederic," I said, "would you like to have a seat? Can I get you some water?"

He nodded. "Water would be nice. Thank you."

"What about me?" Cassandra demanded as

Frederic slumped onto the sofa. "I'd like some water. He's not the only one suffering here."

"Okay," I said. "I'll bring you one, too." I retrieved two bottles of water from the minifridge in my office and gave them to Frederic and Cassandra.

"Thank you," Frederic repeated. "I needed this." He twisted the cap off the bottle and drank deeply.

Cassandra dropped her bottle into her purse. "So, they said at the station that the gems Francesca gave us were real. When are we getting those back?"

"We've taken them into evidence, and you won't be able to get them back until the case is concluded," Ted said.

"You've got to be kidding me! Those are ours! They're going on my wedding gown, and my wedding is taking place in less than two weeks. If I don't have my gown finished by then, I'll be suing someone." She whirled around, prepared to prance back out of the shop.

"Wait," Ted said. "We'll need to question the two of you further."

"Right now?" Cassandra asked over her shoulder. "If you hadn't noticed, we were leaving."

Frederic still sat on the sofa. He sighed and looked up at the ceiling.

A muscle worked in Ted's jaw, and I could tell he was agitated.

Detective Sloan stared at Frederic with unmasked sympathy. I was surprised. So far, she hadn't struck me as the sympathetic type.

"Will you question them together or separately?" I asked.

"Separately." Ted frowned, obviously wondering what I was up to.

"Then maybe you could take Cassandra to the station, and Frederic could go over to MacKenzies' Mochas and unwind for a few minutes before meeting you there," I said.

Cassandra's head whipped in my direction. "What? Now you're wanting Frederic to yourself? All of a sudden, you find out the jewels are real, and you think you'll cozy up to my fiancé? I don't think so!"

"She's not trying to cozy up to me, Cass," Frederic said. "The woman is simply trying to give me a break, okay? God knows I need one!"

"I think that's a good idea," Ted said. "Ms. Wainwright, let's take you down to the station. Mr. Ortega, can you come on down in about an hour?"

Frederic nodded. "Yeah. Thanks."

"I can't believe this! And I'm taking my car. You can come back and get him. Or maybe she'll bring him." Cassandra glared at me. "You're fired!" She sputtered and blustered all the way out onto the street.

"A word in private, please, Ms. Singer?" Ted asked.

"I'll go outside and try to calm Ms. Wainwright," Detective Sloan said.

Ted and I stepped into the office. I gave him my best look of innocence.

He placed his hands lightly on my shoulders as his lips curved into a grin. "I know you, Inch-High Private Eye. What are you up to?"

I shrugged. "Nothing. Don't you think he needs a break from that shrew for a few minutes?"

"You sure you're not cozying up to the guy because those jewels are real?" he teased.

I playfully slapped his arm. "Stop it."

"Be careful, all right? I don't think Frederic Ortega killed his mother, but—"

"I know," I interrupted. "Everyone's a suspect. Go."

"I'll call you tonight," Ted said.

We stepped out of the office. Frederic was still sitting on the sofa, and he looked as if he were dozing.

"Mr. Ortega?" Ted asked.

Frederic started at the sound. "Yes, sir?"

"We'll see you at the station in an hour," Ted said. "You have transportation?"

"I'll call a cab," Frederic said.

"We can send a car for you if you'll give us a call and let us know where you are." Ted gave me a very official-looking nod before he left.

"Frederic," I said, "let me call Sadie at MacKenzies' Mochas and order you some lunch. Either she can bring it over or I'll go get it. You can just rest here for a little while if you'd like."

"Actually, I would like that," he said. "Cass doesn't seem to understand that I lost my mother this morning." His voice broke and he dropped his head into his hands.

"I'm sure she does," I lied. Actually, I wasn't convinced Cassandra Wainwright understood anything. I moved a box of tissues from the counter to the coffee table in front of Frederic. As he quietly wept, I moved over and patted his shoulder. I felt awkward, since I didn't know this man at all. But his mother had been killed outside my shop mere hours ago, and all his fiancée seemed to care about was her wedding gown.

The bells over the door jingled and two of the high school girls from my candlewicking class—Carlie and Jennica—came in. Both were short—though taller than me—with blond hair. Carlie had a shy, dimpling smile, and Jennica's eyes always sparkled with curiosity and speculation.

"Hi, guys," I said, hopping up from the sofa and hurrying over to see what I could help them with. "Are you looking for some embroidery floss?"

"We mainly just came to check on you," Carlie said. "We heard what happened this morning. Everybody's talking about it."

I started shaking my head, but they didn't catch my drift.

"Yeah," Jennica said. "We heard at school that somebody stabbed—"

"Speaking of school," I said quickly, "why aren't you there?"

Carlie laughed. "We got out early today. They're having teacher conferences or something."

"Yeah. I think it's really that the teachers just wanted a break from us," Jennica said.

"Imagine that," I said.

Jennica nodded at Frederic. "What's with that guy?"

I ushered them out the door. "We'll talk in class, okay?"

"Sure. Okay." Carlie looked at Jennica and shrugged.

Once I had the two of them out on the street with the door closed behind us, I whispered, "It was that guy's mother who got stabbed."

Jennica and Carlie looked at each other and then at me. Carlie's mouth formed an O.

"Wow," Jennica said flatly.

"Like I said, we'll talk in class."

The girls walked off down the street, talking excitedly. I went back into the Seven-Year Stitch.

"I'm so sorry about that," I said to Frederic.

"It's all right," he said. "I'm aware people are talking . . . curious . . . and, of course, they're concerned about you." He was holding a tissue he'd used to wipe his eyes. "Do you have a trash can I could drop this in?"

I held out my hand, and he gave me the tissue. I walked around the counter and put the tissue in the trash. "Have you thought about what you might like for lunch? MacKenzies' makes some great sandwiches. My favorite is the chicken salad croissant."

"I'll have one of those. Will you join me?"

"Sure." I took out my cell phone, called Sadie, and ordered two chicken salad croissants.

"Two?" Sadie asked. "You must be starving."

"Something like that," I said. "I'll be over to get them in about fifteen minutes."

Sadie and I said our good-byes, but I could tell she was still wondering why I was ordering two croissants. I'd explain it to her when I picked up the sandwiches.

"I've got sodas in the minifridge," I said. "Would you like one?"

"No. I'm still good with the water," Frederic said.

"Be right back." I hurried into the office and grabbed a diet cola before returning to sit on the sofa across from Frederic.

"I saw her," he said quietly. "Her face, anyway. The coroner had me confirm her identity."

"I'm so sorry."

"She—the coroner—said it happened very quickly. She doesn't think Mom suffered at all," he said. "She said Mom died almost instantly. A moment of shock and then nothing."

I had no idea what to say to Frederic, so I just sat there quietly. Maybe my being there would be some consolation in itself.

"I still can't believe those jewels were real." He ran his hands down his face. "It has to be a mistake. When I talk with the police later, I'm going to ask them to get the gems appraised again. Mom didn't have that kind of money." He reached for another tissue. "She'd recently been fired from a job she'd worked at for more than twenty years." He shook his head in disgust. "She'd worked so hard for this jerk in California. And he ended up firing her for practically no reason whatsoever. She was going to have to live with Cass and me. I mean, she'd already moved here to Tallulah Falls, but she couldn't afford to keep her apartment anymore." He dabbed at his damp eyes. "You know what reason he gave for firing her? She'd cleaned off his desk and put some papers she'd found into his desk drawer. He accused her of snooping . . . invading his privacy."

"After twenty years?" I asked.

"Yeah . . . well, she'd worked for his dad for the first eighteen," Frederic said. "I think he just wanted some new blood. He probably had some girlfriend who needed a job or something."

"Probably. What type of work did your mother do?"

"She was an administrative assistant." He

smiled slightly. "She was good at it. She was a total perfectionist."

"Was perfectionism a common bond between her and Cassandra?"

Frederic barked out a laugh. "Hardly. Mom insists—insisted—on doing everything herself. Cass wants everyone else to do everything for her."

"How did the two of you meet?"

"Up until a few months ago, I worked for the same company as my mom—the Santiago Corporation. The dad—Caleb Santiago Sr.—sort of took me under his wing as a favor to my mom," he said. "I started in the mail room and worked my way up. The company was an office supply sales retailer, and I moved up to regional manager. I met Cass when I was recruiting business from her dad's law firm."

"You said you were with the Santiago Corporation until recently," I said. "Why did you leave?"

He shrugged. "I didn't like the way Caleb Jr. was running things. I got sick of it, acquired a job with another company, and left. Mom stayed. She wasn't happy working there, either, but she had a vested interest and all that. As it turned out, though, the Santiagos pulled that rug out from under her, too."

"Let me run next door and get the sandwiches. I'll be right back." I hated to cut Frederic off at this point in his conversation, but I didn't want Sadie running in with the sandwiches and asking awkward questions, either.

I hurried to MacKenzies' Mochas to pick up and pay for the sandwiches.

"I guess David is keeping you company?" Blake asked. He tried to keep the negative tone out of his voice, but he failed.

"No. It's Frederic Ortega," I said. "The police are questioning Cassandra, and he's going to join her at the station in a little while. He's really having a rough time."

Blake nodded, his relief that the other sandwich wasn't for David evident on his expressive face. "I can imagine."

"And Cassandra isn't being very sympathetic."

"I can imagine that, too," he said. "Did he say anything about . . . you know, about his mom?"

"He said the coroner told him his mother didn't suffer," I said.

"That's good . . . I mean, all things considered."

I nodded and handed Blake some money for the sandwiches. He tried not to take it, but I insisted. Then I rushed back to the shop.

Frederic was on his cell phone finishing up a call. "He must have been watching for her . . . following her or something. They said he struck one definitive blow with the knife, and she went down."

I set the bag on the coffee table as quietly as I could.

"Probably not until Monday or Tuesday," Frederic said. "I still have to make all the arrangements. When will you be here? . . . Good. See you then." He looked at me as he ended the call. "My brother."

"Where does he live?" I asked.

"New Mexico. He'll be here Saturday." He nodded toward the bag. "Those croissants smell good. May I?"

"Of course."

He dug into the bag, setting one croissant and bag of sea salted potato chips on the table for me and putting the other in front of himself. "I didn't realize how hungry I was until I smelled these." He unwrapped the croissant. "Have you ever lost someone close to you, Marcy?"

"My dad," I said. "I was too young when he died to remember much about him, but I can recall his smile . . . and his laugh. He laughed a lot."

"Mom laughed a lot, too," Frederic said, "though not so much in the past year as she used to."

"She seemed to approve of your marriage to Cassandra," I said. "So that's good."

"She'd come to terms with it. Let's put it that way." He bit into the croissant. "You were right. This is good."

She'd come to terms with it. I took that to mean that Francesca hadn't approved of the union at first. I wondered why, but then I remembered he was marrying Cassandra. What mother would want her son shackled to that piece of work? Or herself, for that matter, if she was going to live with the couple?

"Are you planning on calling Mr. Santiago?" I asked. "The one your mother worked with for eighteen years, I mean."

"I hadn't really thought about it," Frederic said. "I suppose I should, but I barely had the presence of mind to call Dom. I haven't even called the funeral home yet."

I unwrapped my croissant and started eating. Like Frederic, I hadn't realized how hungry I was until then. I'd only picked at the muffin Sadie had brought me earlier that morning.

Frederic opened his chips. "About Mom and Cass . . . they got along well in the beginning. But when Cass started planning this wedding, she changed."

"I've heard of women turning into the dreaded beast—Bridezilla," I said with a grin.

"You can say that again. I realize her family will be paying for the wedding, but I was taught to be more frugal. Mom raised my brother and me by herself." He ate a chip. "I understand Cass wanting to have a lavish wedding, but I can't help thinking how far some of that money would go on a home."

"I can understand your point. My own mom put quite a bit of money into my wedding, and then it didn't happen." I shook my head. "There we were with the gorgeous dress, the flowers, the cake, the catered meal, the band . . . and no groom. It was such a waste." My anger at David sparked all over again.

"Whoa," Frederic said. "I'm sorry."

"Yeah, well . . . it happens."

"Cass thinks we can still get married on Valentine's Day, but I don't see that happening now," he said. "Dom and I will have to bury Mom next week. It's just too soon. I . . . I can't get married while I'm still grieving the loss of my mother."

"I understand," I said.

"Maybe you do. But will Cass?"

I didn't say so, but I highly doubted it.

Chapter Seven

Frederic called for a cab rather than have the police station send a car for him. I can't say that I blamed him. I'd much rather leave my shop in a cab than in a squad car. Nellie Davis, who owned the aromatherapy shop down the street, would simply adore seeing me escorted from the premises by an officer. She'd repeatedly voiced her opinion that all my "bad luck" was detrimental for the business of the shopping center in general. Frankly, my shop was doing well, thank you very much.

I remembered seeing David in Nellie's shop prior to his coming to the Seven-Year Stitch—when I still thought maybe I was imagining things. It made me wonder if Nellie had somehow found out about David and persuaded him to come here and take me back to California. I realized that was a stretch; but when a murder takes place just outside your shop—especially after two others have been linked to your shop in some way—you begin to get a little paranoid.

I decided to call Mom and tell her the latest.

"Hi," I said when she answered the phone. "What are you doing?"

"Finishing up my packing for New York," she said. "What are you doing?"

"I just had lunch with the man whose mother was stabbed to death outside my shop this morning." As soon as I said that, I held the phone away from my ear because I knew I'd regret it if I didn't.

"You what!" she shrieked. "Is this some kind of a joke? Because if it is, Marcella Singer, I swear I'll—"

"No joke, Mom." I explained to her about Francesca Ortega. "Remember those fake gems I told you she'd wanted me to use to embellish Cassandra's wedding gown? The police had them appraised, and they weren't fake."

"And the killer knew that?"

"Maybe. I know he killed her with one blow, and no one seems to have heard or seen anything," I said.

"Was she stabbed in the front or in the back?" she asked.

"Front. Why?"

"Then she didn't know her attacker," Mom said. "Had she known the person, she'd have been afraid and reacted—turned to run or something. She thought the person was simply passing her on the street, and then he stabbed her."

"Unless it was someone she wasn't afraid of. Frederic told me his mother had lost her job and was going to be living with him and Cassandra. I don't think Cassandra would have been very pleased about that," I said.

"Still, that's no reason to kill her. Just because Cassandra is a drama queen with a venomous attitude doesn't mean she's a killer. Of course, it doesn't mean that she's not, either." Mom sighed. "Let me hang up and cancel my flight to New York and schedule one to—"

"No way," I interrupted. "You missed enough work because of me the last time you came for an unscheduled visit. I'm fine."

"But—"

"No buts. Sadie, Todd, and Ted are looking out for me. And, of course, right now David is, too." I paused. "Mom, do you think he deserves a second chance?"

"I've already told you, love, you're the only one who can answer that question."

"But I don't want to get it wrong. Like today when Ms. Ortega was found stabbed to death outside my shop, I began to think maybe I should get back together with David and come home to San Francisco."

"One," said Mom, "you don't have to get back

with David in order to come back to San Francisco. You know I'd love to have you back home, but don't make that decision when you're stressed out. Two, don't run scared. From or to anything. You'll regret it if you do. If you're thinking of giving David a second chance, don't commit to anything until after this business is resolved and you're thinking clearly again."

"You're right."

"I'm always right. It's because I'm old."

I laughed. "You are not old."

"Okay. I'm experienced," she said. "I will tell you this much. I don't know about David, but I know that you have grown and changed since you and he dated last. Don't let the past completely influence your decision. Try to see him with fresh eyes."

"I will. Thanks, Mom."

"You're sure you don't need me to come to Tallulah Falls?" she asked. "I can be there in two shakes of a lamb's tail. Okay, probably more like a few thousand shakes of a lamb's tail, but you get my meaning."

"I'm fine. I'll keep you posted."

"You'd better."

As I was hanging up the phone, a customer came in for some cross-stitch canvas. I led her over to the canvases and pointed out some new flosses I'd just gotten in. She bought two canvas sheets and a few skeins of floss before leaving.

Afterward, I sat in the sit-and-stitch square and thought about Frederic and his mother. I wondered if the senior Santiago—the one Francesca had worked for all those years—had known his son was giving her such a bad deal. Maybe if he knew about Francesca's death, he and Frederic could talk. With David sauntering back into my life, I understood all too well about the need for closure and having unanswered questions put to rest.

I went into the office, pulled up a search engine on the computer, and typed in *Santiago Corporation*. The company was one of the first listed for discount office supplies. I clicked on the company's Web site and saw tabs for ink, furniture, technology, paper, and general supplies.

I scrolled to the bottom of the page and saw *About Us*. I clicked that link. There was a photo of Caleb Santiago Jr. and his brother, Nicholas. They were in a warehouse. One held a clipboard, and both were smiling at the camera. They were wearing dress shirts, ties, jeans, and hard hats. It was obvious the photo was meant to show that these two megawealthy young men were "regular guys," people you could trust with your business. Caleb had straight, dark brown hair while Nicholas's was wavy and black, but both had athletic builds, brown eyes, and friendly faces. I'd buy office products from these people.

I tried to see something sinister in Caleb's countenance, but I couldn't. Maybe he had caught Francesca snooping. After all, I didn't know the Ortegas well enough to make a judgment call. Francesca—and her son, too, for that matter—seemed nice, but that didn't mean they really were. Or maybe Francesca was merely loyal to the senior Santiago and was snooping in Caleb's office for his father. What if the dad had asked Francesca to make sure his son was running the company appropriately?

I read the paragraph giving the history of the company. Caleb Santiago Sr.'s father had started the company in 1962. Caleb had taken over the reins when his father retired, and Caleb Jr.—the elder Santiago son—had likewise taken over when Caleb Sr. retired. The paragraph related the story of how the first Santiago had begun selling high-quality pens door to door. Today the business was conducted primarily online, but customer representatives were always on hand to take your calls. Sometimes, they still even visited their customers in person. Yadda, yadda, yadda.

Gee, what a happy place. It was like Disneyland with staplers and toner cartridges. I half expected to see where Caleb Santiago Sr.'s head had been cryogenically frozen, but then it didn't appear he was dead yet. I wondered what he'd have to say about Francesca Ortega.

I called the toll-free number, and tried to get an office number for Mr. Santiago. No dice. The heavily accented telephone operator told me she was not allowed to give out information for the home office but that she would be happy to help me place my order. I thanked her and hung up.

I then did a search for Caleb Santiago's attorney. With that search, I hit gold and came up with the name Gilbert Carroll. I called Mr. Carroll's office and indicated I'd like to speak with him about a former employee of Mr. Santiago. I told the receptionist that Ms. Ortega had died this morning and that I believed she'd been a longtime employee of Mr. Santiago's company. The receptionist took my name and number and said she'd pass my message along to Mr. Carroll.

Given the receptionist's dismissive attitude, I doubted I'd get a call back from Mr. Carroll. Imagine my surprise when I got a return phone call—not from Mr. Carroll, but from Caleb Santiago Sr. himself.

"Is this Marcy Singer?" Mr. Santiago asked when I answered the phone.

"Yes, it is," I said.

"This is Caleb Santiago Sr. I understand you called my attorney's office and told them that Francesca Ortega had passed away this morning."

"Yes, sir, I did."

"I wasn't aware she'd been ill," he said.

"She was stabbed," I said.

He was quiet for a moment, and then he said, "That can't be. Who'd want to hurt Frannie?"

"It appears she was killed during a robbery. Her purse was missing."

"Stabbed to death? During a robbery, you say? That's horrible. Where are you located?"

"Tallulah Falls, Oregon," I said. "It's on the coast."

"And it's known for being a rough area?" he asked.

"No. Generally, this is a peaceful, low-crime area."

"Thank you for your call, Ms. Singer," he said. "I'll give Frederic a call later this evening to express my condolences to him personally and to find out about the arrangements. Again, I appreciate that you let me know."

"You're welcome, Mr. Santiago. I'm sorry about Ms. Ortega."

"So am I," he said. "Terribly sorry."

"I understand that she worked for you for a long time," I said.

"Eighteen years." He sighed. "Good day, Ms. Singer."

So now he was going to call Frederic. I wondered if I should've butted in where I had no business. But I wanted so badly to speak with the Santiagos about Francesca. It was apparent Mr. Santiago had thought highly of her, but what about his sons? Did Caleb Jr. catch Francesca snooping through his desk? Or was Frederic right and the young man simply had someone else in mind for Francesca's job? And where did Francesca get those gemstones?

The rest of the day passed without much excitement. Of course, I hadn't expected it to get any more exciting than it had been this morning, but it was slower than I'd anticipated it being. There were a few customers in and out of the shop that afternoon, and class went well that evening. After we dispensed with the news about the morning robbery outside the shop, we were able to get down to stitching. Surprisingly, I hadn't heard anything more from Sadie, Todd, Ted, or David throughout the day.

After class, I took Angus outside for a walk before the short drive home. Back inside, I was straightening up the sit-and-stitch square when Todd came in. Angus ran to greet him as I fluffed a pillow and returned it to one of the sofas.

"Hi, there," I said with a smile.

"Hi, yourself." Todd grinned. "Suddenly, I'm seeing you in a little French maid uniform."

"Don't go there," I warned.

He laughed. "All right, all right. It's just odd to see you being so . . . domesticated."

"What's that supposed to mean? I run an embroidery store, for Pete's sake!"

"I know. I mean, it's odd to see you cleaning," he said.

I put my hands on my hips. "So now I'm a slob?"

"Should I go out, come back in again, and start all over?"

I cocked my head. "You don't have to go back out, because it's cold out there. But starting all over is a good idea."

"Okay." Todd cleared his throat. "Why, good evening, Ms. Singer. I'm here to escort you home."

"That's better," I said. "Although you are kinda going overboard with the formality and the offer to escort me home."

"Actually, I'm serious about that. I'm going to see you to your car and follow you home."

"Follow me home?" I asked. "And I guess you'll expect me to keep you?"

His smiled broadened. "That's the plan."

I laughed. "Thank you. It isn't necessary, you know. But I appreciate your concern."

"It is necessary. I'd like to get some sleep tonight, and I couldn't without knowing I saw you safely home." He patted the side of his leg. "Angus, you wanna ride with me?"

Angus jumped around Todd, obviously excited at the thought of going with him.

"Be that way," I told them.

"Aw, now, you know we're just going to talk about you," Todd said. "How sweet you are . . . what a lousy driver . . ."

He laughed as I picked up the pillow I'd just fluffed and hit him on the head with it.

"Don't tear that up," he said. "I can't make you another one."

"No," I said, hitting him again. "But I can."

"In that case . . ." He picked up another pillow and began hitting me back.

Angus barked, wanting to join in our play. He ran and got his tug toy and dropped it at Todd's feet.

"You are a total traitor, Mr. Angus O'Ruff," I said. "First you want to ride home with Todd, and now you're letting him wail on me with a pillow?"

"He knows you started it." Todd patted Angus' head and picked up the tug toy. "Come on. You wanna play? I'll play tug-of-war with you."

As they engaged in their match, I finished tidying up the shop. Then I got on my coat and grabbed my purse.

"Ready?" I asked.

"Ready," Todd said, dropping the tug toy and taking Angus' leash from off the counter. "Let's go, boy."

I turned off the lights, and we stepped out onto the sidewalk. As I locked the door, I glanced over to where Francesca's body had lain, and shivered.

Todd placed a hand on my shoulder. "Don't look at it. I'll get that cleaned up as soon as I can."

"Oh no," I said, "I'll do it." I turned to him and frowned. "Come to think of it, I thought the police would do it when they were finished examining the crime scene."

He shook his head. "I'm afraid not. But I'll see what I can do. I'll talk with Ted first and make sure they're done."

"Thank you."

As Todd walked me to my Jeep, a patrol car slowly drove past. There was another one driving down my street when we arrived home.

Todd gave a dubious snort when he noticed the car. "He might have the patrol officers looking out for you, but he didn't provide you with an escort home."

"Duly noted," I said. Indeed, it seemed everyone was concerned about my safety this evening except for David. His presence, phone calls, text messages, even e-mails were conspicuously absent.

As promised, Ted called to check on me later Thursday night.

"I just got off the phone with Todd Calloway," he said. "He asked if he could clean up the sidewalk in front of the Seven-Year Stitch. I told him he could, so hopefully he'll get that done before you go in to work tomorrow morning."

"Thank you," I said. "I'll have to thank Todd, too."

"I guess so. He told me he escorted you home."

"We saw the extra patrol cars around the shop and house," I said. "I appreciate that."

"You're welcome. As much as I dislike Todd

sometimes, I'm glad to know he's helping look out for you," Ted said.

"About all this 'looking out for Marcy'—what's up with that?"

"Just a precaution."

"Ted?" My voice warned him to be straight with me.

"We're concerned the thief might come back for the jewels."

"But I gave those to you."

"He might not be aware of that," he said. "I doubt he'd ever come back, but . . . better safe . . . you know." He cleared his throat. "Do you mind if I ask about this Frist guy who claimed to be your fiancé this morning?"

"No, I don't mind. He was my fiancé over a year ago—way before I came to Tallulah Falls—and he stood me up."

"That's the jerk who broke your heart?"

"Yep."

Ted was silent for so long I had to ask if he was still there.

"I'm here," he said. "I'm just trying to figure out something to arrest him for."

I laughed. He didn't.

"I think I might've gotten myself into hot water with Frederic Ortega," I said.

"How so?"

I explained to Ted that Frederic had told me his mother worked for the Santiago Corporation—

and more specifically for Mr. Santiago—for twenty years. "Anyway, I called Mr. Santiago's attorney to let him know about Francesca. Mr. Santiago returned my call, and I told him she'd had been stabbed to death outside my shop."

"Why do you think calling Santiago will get you in trouble with Mr. Ortega?"

"There's bad blood between him and the Santiago son who took over running the company for his dad a couple years ago. The son fired Francesca after accusing her of snooping through his desk. Frederic didn't think the accusation held water, but I'm kind of wondering if it did."

"Because you think maybe she stole the gemstones?" Ted asked.

"Don't you think that's possible? I mean, she either had to somehow obtain real stones when she thought she was getting fake ones, or else she knew what she was getting. I don't know how a woman who'd been fired from her job and was going to have to move in with her son and daughter-in-law in order to make ends meet could afford to buy nearly a hundred thousand dollars' worth of jewels. Do you?"

"No. So Frederic told you his mother was going to move in with him and Cassandra?"

"Yes," I said.

"Maybe Ms. Ortega ordered the hit on herself, then," Ted said.

"The hit?"

Ted sighed. "That slipped out. I did not just say that, okay?"

"Of course you didn't. Now explain."

"Whoever killed Francesca knew exactly what he was doing. He inserted the knife just below the sternum and into the heart. The coroner said the puncture caused an embolism and killed Francesca almost immediately."

"So the murderer knew how to stab Francesca to cause an embolism?" I asked. "Do you think he was a medical professional?"

"No," Ted said. "He couldn't have known the knife wound would cause an embolism. But he—or she—did know exactly where and how to stab Ms. Ortega to make the jab a fatal one. That's what makes me think it was a professional hit."

"Who would order a hit on Francesca Ortega?" I asked.

"My guess would be the person she got the jewels from."

Chapter Eight

Friday morning, Angus and I arrived at the shop an hour earlier than usual. The shop didn't open until ten o'clock, but I wanted to get there in time to work on the sidewalk. I didn't feel right about letting Todd do it alone. When we got there, however, he was just finishing up. When he saw us drive up, he dropped the scrub brush he'd been using into a white bucket and pushed the bucket behind him with his foot.

"Todd, why didn't you call me?" I asked. "I'd have been here sooner."

"We already had the French maid discussion," he said, "and I didn't want to be beaten with a pillow this early in the morning."

"Thank you." I handed him the keys to the shop. "Why don't you unlock the door and take

Angus on in, and I'll go to MacKenzies' and get us some coffee and muffins."

He raised his brows. "Sounds like a plan to me."

"And, in the meantime, I can imagine you in a French maid costume," I said.

"Hey!"

I laughed and darted out of the way as he made a grab for me. "Be right back."

I hurried to MacKenzies' Mochas. Blake was behind the counter.

"You're flushed and breathless," he said. "You didn't jog to work this morning, did you?"

"No," I said, "but I have been standing out in the cold talking with Todd. He cleaned up the sidewalk for me."

"Todd's a good man," he said.

"Yes, he is. Can you make me up a box filled with his favorite muffins and pastries, give me my usual vanilla cinnamon latte, and make whatever Todd usually orders in the mornings?"

Blake nodded. "FYI, he orders an espresso in the mornings—I'm making it a double shot today—and then he switches to dark roast by midmorning."

"Good to know."

Sadie popped around the corner and put an empty serving tray on the counter. "What's good to know?"

"That Todd likes espresso early in the morning," Blake said with a wink at his wife.

"Is there something you guys aren't telling me?" she asked.

"Nope," I said.

She looked out the window. "Your morning is about to get a tad more interesting."

I turned to see Cassandra and Frederic heading toward the Seven-Year Stitch. "I'd say at this point, their morning is about to get more interesting. Todd and Angus are probably going wild playing in the shop right about now. And I've already told you how Cassandra loves Angus."

Sadie giggled. "Take your time on Marcy's order, Blake."

"Oh no," I said. "Please hurry. As sweet as Todd has been to me, I can't leave him and Angus alone with those two. Cassandra fired me yesterday. I can't imagine why she's coming back . . . unless it's to let me know she's suing me or something."

Blake finished making the espresso and the latte while Sadie filled a box with treats she and her husband knew to be Todd's favorites. I paid them and then gathered up my purchases.

"Do you need help with those?" Sadie asked, a twinkle in her eye.

"No, Ms. Nosy. Come over later, and I'll tell you everything."

She laughed. "Count on it."

I walked back up the street, being careful not to drop anything. Todd saw me coming, and he quickly opened the door and took the drinks.

"Thank you," I said. I searched his face for a sign of what Frederic and Cassandra were doing there, but there was no clue. He simply smiled, turned, and strode over to the counter, where he set the drinks.

"Good morning," I said to Frederic and Cassandra. I was surprised to see Angus dropping his tennis ball at Frederic's feet. I set the box on the counter beside the drinks. "Let me hang my coat up, and I'll be right there."

Todd followed me into the office and helped me off with my coat.

"What's up with them?" I whispered.

He shrugged.

"Did either of them mention anything about killing me?" I asked.

"No. And Fred and Angus seem to have bonded over tennis," Todd said.

"This is not funny." I turned to go, but then turned back to Todd. "Thank you again for cleaning up the walk. I'm so glad Frederic didn't have to see . . . you know . . . *that* anymore. You're wonderful."

"Thank me properly after they leave?"

I blushed and went out into the shop. "Is there anything I can get either of you? We have muffins."

"No, thank you," Cassandra said. "We're here because I was a little bit hasty yesterday when I fired you. I was terribly upset over everything that had happened. I'm sure you understand."

"Of course," I said.

"So, I'm hiring you back," she said. "We don't know how soon it will be before we get the gemstones back, but I feel confident it will be in time for you to get the dress finished."

I smiled but didn't respond. After talking with Ted last night, I felt confident that Cassandra wouldn't be getting those gemstones back anytime soon. "I think I owe you an apology, Frederic."

"Why is that?" he asked, tossing the tennis ball for Angus again.

"After speaking with you yesterday, I got in touch with your mother's former employer and told him about her death. I know I way overstepped my bounds, but . . ." I shrugged. "I'm sorry."

"It's okay," Frederic said. "I realize you were only trying to help. Mr. Santiago called me last night, and he's flying here for the funeral on Tuesday. He cared for my mom. He said she'd been a valued friend as well as employee to him over the years."

And yet, he'd allowed his son to fire her. I wondered about that.

"Again, I apologize. I had no right to call him," I said.

He took the ball Angus had returned and tossed it again. "I should've called him myself. There's just so much to think about right now. It's hard to take care of everything."

"Well, we'll be in touch." Cassandra stood and headed for the door. "Frederic, we need to go."

"Yeah." Frederic got up and listlessly followed Cassandra out of the shop.

"Man, that poor guy is pathetic," Todd said. He brought our drinks and the muffins and sat down beside me on the sofa. "And I'm not just talking about his losing his mom."

"It doesn't seem like Cassandra supports him at all, does it?" I asked.

"No. I think Cassandra only cares about supporting herself." He opened the box. "Muffins and bear claws? Oh yeah."

"You said you wanted to be thanked properly," I reminded him.

He chuckled. "Yeeaah. We'll come back to that."

I finally heard from David at about one o'clock Friday afternoon. He called my cell phone. Since both numbers were on my business listing, and since I didn't recognize the number that came up, I answered, "Good afternoon. This is the Seven-Year Stitch. How may I help you?"

"You can help me by telling me where to pick

you up for dinner," David said. "You want me to swing by the shop and get you?"

My stomach roiled. Why had I agreed to dinner? Well, too late now. "No. I need to take Angus home and feed him, retouch my makeup, and all that stuff. Why don't you pick me up there?" I gave him the address, and he said he'd see me around six.

"Is there any place special you'd like to go?" he asked.

"Yeah, there is," I said. "It's a little place in Depoe Bay. It isn't too far from here, and I love it."

"Depoe Bay it is, then."

After we hung up, I tried to gauge my feelings toward my upcoming evening with David. On the one hand, I dreaded it. I still had a lot of hurt and resentment built up over the way he'd treated me the day of our wedding. Those wounds had healed quite a bit, but it wouldn't take much to open them back up.

On the other hand, I wanted to see how I'd feel being on a date with him again. Would I hang on his every word? Would I weigh everything I wanted to say to try to determine how David would react before I spoke? Could he still make me laugh?

The bells above the shop door jingled, and I turned to see who'd come in.

"It's just me," said Sadie. "Don't bother getting

up." She slipped off her jacket, sat down on the sofa facing away from the window, and looked at me. "Are you thinking of investing in an espresso machine?"

I grinned and went back to working on the Kuba cloth quilt. "Should I?"

"You tell me."

"Don't get your hopes up," I said. "Todd was just here when I got to work this morning cleaning up the sidewalk."

"Yeah, I know," she said. "Blake filled me in. You have to admit, though, that was a really thoughtful gesture."

"It was. Todd is a wonderful man," I said.

"I sense a but. There's a but, isn't there?" Sadie lifted her long hair off her shoulders and then let it drop before leaning forward.

"I'm seeing David tonight."

"So there is a but. A big but," she said.

"I have to know, Sadie. I have to be absolutely sure I'm doing the right thing if and when I tell him to get out of my life for good."

"I know you do." She sighed. "Just realize he's going to be on his best behavior tonight."

"It might not be enough," I said. "Right now—being completely honest with myself—if I'm torn between any two men, it's Todd and Ted. They're both terrific, and I could see falling for either one of them if I'd only let myself."

Sadie laughed. "You know I think Todd would

be great for you, but I have to admit you're in a pretty enviable position. It's like you're Kate from *Lost*, and you're in a love triangle with two hot but totally different guys."

I laughed, too. "And now here comes . . . who? What *Lost* character would David be like?"

"The smoke monster!"

After we'd shared a laugh over that, I said, "I'm glad we can talk about all this now. Not too long ago, you'd get angry with me over my feelings for Ted."

"I know. But I came to the conclusion that you're a big girl and I'm not your mother. I can't choose your boyfriends for you. Blake and I love both you and Todd—Todd has been like a brother to Blake—but you have to do what's best for you. If you don't, you'll wind up hurting yourself and everyone else."

"Good point," I said. "And that's why I have to figure out my feelings for David."

"So, what did Cassandra and Frederic want this morning?" she asked.

"Cassandra wanted to unfire me. I accepted the job back because I know she'll never get the jewels back, and I won't be working on that dress ever again. I'm mailing a check for the retainer back to Cassandra and telling her we'll settle the bill after the dress is finished. Confidentially, I'm not sure the wedding will take place, either."

"Really?" Her eyes widened. "Do tell."

"Think about it, Sadie. She wants to get married the week after Frederic buries his mother. She hasn't backed off from that yet—at least, not that I know of. Wouldn't you offer to postpone the wedding for a month or two if you were in her position?"

"Yeah, I would. You would. Any reasonable person would. Cassandra Wainwright is not a reasonable person."

"I feel sorry for Frederic," I said. "You're Tallulah Falls's resident matchmaker. Can't you come up with someone new for Frederic?"

She tilted her head. "Give me a day or two to mull that over."

At five o'clock that afternoon, I closed up the shop and took Angus home. I ran upstairs and turned on the water in the bathtub. While the tub was filling, I hurried back downstairs and gave Angus his dinner.

I bathed and slipped into my robe to apply my makeup and fix my hair. I took special care with my makeup, and I curled my hair so that it fell in soft waves around my face. Yes, I had mixed feelings about this date—but one thing I did know: I wanted David to feel as rotten as possible about leaving me at the altar.

I didn't want to overdress since we were going to the diner, so I put on black trousers and a red silk shirt. A gray leather blazer would complete the outfit nicely. I went down and let Angus into the backyard before David arrived.

I heard the doorbell, checked my appearance in the hall mirror, and opened the door. As expected, it was David.

"You look fantastic," he said.

"Thanks," I said. "You look nice, too." He wore brown dress pants, a light blue button-down shirt, and a camel sport coat.

He came inside, shut the door with his heel, and pulled me to him for a kiss. I put my hands on his arms and tried to reciprocate, but I'd been caught off guard. His touch felt both familiar and foreign to me. I pulled away.

"We should get to Depoe Bay ahead of the crowd," I said.

"Yeah. I guess we should. Nice place," David said. "I could live here."

My eyes widened. I didn't recall issuing an invitation.

"Of course, that would have to go."

I turned to see what he was talking about. I couldn't see what he meant. If he meant anything in my living room, I was guessing it would be him. I loved my living room. It was open and airy, had a huge picture window, an inviting fireplace . . . "What would have to go?"

"That white furniture." He nodded toward my overstuffed sofa. "Isn't it a pain to keep clean?"

"Not for me, it isn't. I love it."

"You would." He shook his head. "Let's go."

On the drive to Depoe Bay, I struggled to find something to talk about. Other than the fact that my white furniture was none of his concern.

"You said you've been out of work," I said. "You were laid off from the company where you worked when we met?"

"Nah," he said. "I've worked at a couple places since we broke up. None of them have really been me, you know?"

"It can be hard to find your niche sometimes."

"Yeah, you got lucky. You had a rich mom to help you get started in whatever you wanted to do," he said.

"My mom didn't help me get started here," I said, trying not to grind my teeth. "I opened my shop, bought my house, and did everything here on my own."

"Well, good for you, then. But, still, you knew she'd be right there if you needed her."

He was right—Mom would have been there had I needed her. But I didn't like his tone, so I just didn't respond to that comment.

"So, what's the deal with the beer guy?" David asked. "Is that who you've been seeing since you've been here?"

"I've gone on a few dates with Todd."

"And what's his deal? Is he pretty well off?"

"I don't know," I said. "Todd and I don't typically discuss our finances with each other."

"Just asking. Gee. Don't get so defensive." He took my hand.

Frankly, I'd have preferred him to keep both hands on the wheel, especially since he was being so obnoxious. Had he always been like this?

At last we were there.

"That's it up ahead," I said.

"Captain Moe's?" David asked. "It doesn't look like much more than a greasy spoon."

"It's a small diner," I said, "but the food—and the proprietor—is terrific."

"Apparently, looks really can be deceiving, then, because it looks like a dive." David got out of the car and came around and opened the door for me.

We made our way through the already-crowded parking lot. David held the door as I stepped into the diner.

Captain Moe was behind the counter. "Well, look what the cat dragged in! It's a wee little mouse."

I giggled as Captain Moe came around the counter to hug me. Captain Moe is a bear of a man who reminds me of Alan Hale, who played the hefty, white-haired Skipper on *Gilligan's Island*. Only Captain Moe has a beard and the heartiest laugh I've ever heard.

"Captain Moe, this is David Frist," I said. "He's a friend visiting me from San Francisco."

"Pleasure to meet you, David," Captain Moe said, extending a beefy hand.

"Nice to meet you, too," David said, shaking Captain Moe's hand.

"Speaking of San Fran, how's your mother, Marcy?" Captain Moe asked.

"She's fine. She's heading for New York to another movie set," I said.

He stroked his neatly trimmed white beard. "Wonder if she could get me a bit part in one of those films. I'll have to ask the next time she's in town." He looked at David. "So, what do you do, young man? Are you in the movie business, too?"

"I'm not in any business at the moment," David said, looking around the restaurant. "Should we wait to be seated, or can we just grab that empty table over there?"

"Help yourself," Captain Moe said. He arched a brow at me, and I shrugged slightly.

"Captain Moe makes the best burgers on the coast," I told David. "You should try one."

"Yep, that's what Tink always has." Captain Moe winked.

"Tink?" David asked.

I laughed. "He and his brother both call me Tinkerbell. I'm not sure whether they're referring to my height or my mischievous charm."

"I'll not touch that one, my dear," Captain Moe

said. "Will you be having a burger, too, David? If so, I'll go ahead and have the cook get started on them."

"Yeah, I guess," David said.

"All right, then. Sit yourselves down, and I'll be out in a few." Captain Moe headed for the kitchen.

"You have some strange friends here in Oregon," David said.

I decided that was a good thing. I was starting to dislike my "friends" from San Francisco.

Chapter Nine

I was between customers late Saturday morning and was dozing off on a chair in the sit-and-stitch square when my phone rang. I jerked upright, glad the needle I'd been holding while working on the Kuba cloth quilt wasn't a sharp one. I hadn't slept well at all last night, and I was having trouble keeping my eyes open.

"Seven-Year Stitch," I answered.

"Hi, Marcy. It's Riley."

Riley Kendall was a friend who happened at the moment to be a pregnant attorney on bed rest. She also happened to be Captain Moe's niece.

"How're you feeling?" I asked.

"Bored. I did get an interesting call from Uncle Moe this morning, though. He said you were at the diner with a total jerk last night."

"Leave it to Captain Moe to call 'em like he sees

'em." I explained about my former fiancé coming in from San Francisco and wanting me to get back together with him. "So I went on a date with him to see how that would pan out."

"And how did it?" Riley asked.

"Right after we ate, I told David I had a headache and asked him to take me home. Riley, he was awful. And I don't know if he was always that awful and I was simply blind to it, or if this awfulness is something new."

"I imagine he was always a jerk and you couldn't see it because you cared about him. You don't care about him anymore—or, at least, there's some distance between you and your former feelings—so you can better see him for what he is."

"Wow. That was kinda deep," I said.

"Yeah, well, I'm a lawyer. I can come up with crap like that right off the cuff." She laughed. "But, in your case—and given what Uncle Moe said—I think it's true. He didn't care for your date at all. And Uncle Moe tries to see the best in everyone."

"I know. David was totally obnoxious last night. And it didn't just come about gradually. He was like that from the moment he walked through my front door. It was as if he and I had nothing in common whatsoever. I couldn't even find anything to talk to him about anymore. I would say it was like we were total strangers, but I can usually make conversation with strangers."

"Did you tell this guy to go back to California and never come back?" she asked.

"Not yet. I pretty much just wanted to get last night over with before dealing with another drama." I blew out a breath. "You can't believe the week I've had."

"Yeah, I know. I've been trying to keep up with you—and everyone else—through the newspapers and the grapevine. I should've called you before now. Do the police have any leads on whoever stabbed that woman outside your shop?"

"No. And that whole situation keeps getting weirder and weirder." I told Riley about the gemstones Francesca had given Cassandra and Frederic to go on the wedding gown. "I—and I think Cassandra and Frederic—thought they were fake. But it turned out they were real. After Francesca's death, Frederic confided to me about his mother losing the job she'd held for twenty years and what dire financial straits she'd found herself in."

"So, where'd she get the jewels?" Riley asked.

"That's the mystery." I explained how the junior Santiago had fired Francesca on the basis that he'd caught her snooping through his desk. "Now, apparently, the senior Santiago seemed to think very highly of Francesca, and yet he allowed his son to fire her."

"Do you think she stole the gems from the Santiagos?"

"I don't know. But there has to be a reason that

Mr. Santiago spoke so highly of Francesca but still allowed her to lose her job," I said. "I mean, it was his company. He must still have some clout. Had he wanted her to stay with the company—even in a different capacity—wouldn't he have been given his way?"

"Santiago," Riley mused. "Why is that name ringing a bell?"

"I don't know. Do you buy your office supplies online from the Santiago Corporation?"

"No, that's not it. Wait a sec." I heard her riffling through papers on the other end of the phone line. "Here it is. It was in the newspaper a couple days ago. The Santiago Corporation's chief executive officer, Caleb Santiago Jr., is going to be in Toledo Saturday afternoon for a meeting at the Grand Mountain Lodge with potential investors. It says here that the investors are trying to bring new businesses—including a branch of the Santiago Corporation—to the Toledo area."

"Toledo. That's only about half an hour from here, right?" I asked.

"*Um* . . . I don't think just anyone can attend the meeting, if that's what you're thinking."

"No, but anyone can visit the hotel and wait for Mr. Santiago to go into or come out of the meeting. What time will he be there?"

"The dinner meeting is to take place at five o'clock p.m. in the main conference room," Riley read.

"If I close up the shop an hour early, I could get there before he goes into the meeting," I said. "Maybe he'll agree to talk with me either before or after the meeting."

"Good luck. Keep me posted. This bed rest thing is killing me. I'll be thrilled to do whatever I can to help . . . using my laptop and phone, of course."

"Thanks, Riley."

The phone call from Riley woke me up a little bit, although I think the prospect of going to Toledo and trying to see Caleb Santiago Jr. perked me up even more. I needed to find out the deal with those jewels and try to determine who had ordered Francesca to be killed.

I put away the Kuba cloth quilt and pulled up my phone's navigational system. I was more used to traveling north than south since I'd been here in Oregon. I pulled up the browser to get an address for the Grand Mountain Lodge, and then typed in that address to get driving directions and an estimate for the amount of time it would take me to get to the lodge. Within seconds, a map popped up with detailed directions and the prediction that it would take me thirty-eight minutes to reach the lodge from here.

I glanced up to see David open the door for a customer before coming into the store himself.

"Good morning," he said. "No need to call me, because here I am." He laughed.

I smiled stiffly and stood to greet both him and the customer. "Good morning." I placed my phone on the counter and approached the customer. "I'm Marcy Singer. Is there anything I can help you with?"

"Nice to meet you, Marcy. I'm Cheryl, and I'm looking for either a crochet or knitting how-to kit," the woman said. She appeared to be in her early to midfifties, had light brown hair styled to perfection, and had a pleasant smile. "I'm getting ready to become a grandmother for the very first time, and I'd like to be able to either knit or crochet the baby a blanket."

"That's wonderful! Congratulations!" I led Cheryl to the knitting and crocheting section. "Some people seem to think crocheting is easier and that it goes faster than knitting. If you have a few minutes, I can teach you some basic stitches for either one."

"Really? That'd be great. Can you get me started with crochet?" she asked.

"Sure. What color yarn would you like to use?"

She tilted her head as she examined the colors of yarn I had in the bins. "What about yellow? I think that would be pretty."

"Yellow it is." I picked up a skein of yellow yarn, a medium-size crochet hook, and a pattern book. "Let's go over here to the seating area."

I led the woman to the sit-and-stitch square

where David had sat down on the sofa facing away from the window. He shot me an impatient look, but I refused to be intimidated. After all, this was my business. I was at work doing what I was supposed to be doing.

"Let's start with the chain stitch." I showed Cheryl how to make the stitch and then watched her face light up with delight as she made a row of joined loops.

"This is fun!" she said. She smiled at me and then at David, who grinned tightly in return.

After she'd mastered the chain stitch, I showed Cheryl how to do the slip stitch and the yarn over stitch.

"Let's find a pattern you like, so I can be sure to show you the stitches you'll need to know in order to complete your grandchild's blanket," I said, opening the pattern book.

We found a baby blanket pattern for beginners. It called for single crochet, V-stitch, and double crochet stitches.

It took us about an hour, but by the time Cheryl left, she had nearly one-fourth of her blanket completed. She paid for her yarn, hook, and pattern book and thanked me for my assistance.

"I feel confident you'll be able to finish the blanket on your own," I said, "but if you need any more help, you know where to find me."

"I sure do. Thanks again, Marcy. You've been a tremendous help to me this morning."

Cheryl left, and I turned to David with a huge smile. David looked irritated.

"Wasn't that great?" I asked.

"It was pretty rude, if you want my opinion. You could've excused yourself, found out what I wanted, and then helped her," he said.

"I guess I could have done that. But during work hours, customers come first except in an emergency." I sat back down on the sofa across from the one where David sat. "Do you have an emergency?"

"No. I just wanted to find out what time we're going out tonight, and if we can go somewhere decent this time."

"Actually, I have other plans tonight. I'm closing the shop early and driving to Toledo," I said.

"Toledo, Ohio?" he asked.

I rolled my eyes. "Toledo, Oregon. It's not all that far from here."

"What's in Toledo?"

"The Grand Mountain Lodge," I said.

The bells over the shop door jingled. I glanced up, but David didn't seem to notice.

"So, who's getting the all-nighter?" He sneered. "Beer boy?"

Since it was Todd who'd entered the shop, he took this as his cue. "Good morning, darling," he said, his rich voice reverberating throughout the store. "Beer boy at your service." He came over and sat down beside me on the sofa, draping an arm across my shoulders. "What did you tell Dave here about our all-nighter, beer girl?"

I pressed my lips together to keep from laughing. "I didn't tell him anything. Do you want to explain about our trip to the Grand Mountain Lodge?"

"I'd be delighted." He leaned forward, eager to spin his yarn. I was looking forward to hearing it myself.

Angus came up and placed his head on Todd's knee. Even he couldn't wait to hear this!

Scratching Angus behind the ears, Todd began his tale. "Grand Mountain is one of the ritziest hotels around here. I thought we'd start with a nice dinner." He winked at David. "Gotta keep up our strength, you know. Then we'll dance for a couple hours in the main ballroom . . . have some wine . . . maybe some strawberries dipped in chocolate." He looked at me.

"Sounds great," I said.

David stood, his eyes spitting venom at me. "After the way you treated me last night—acting all frigid when we kissed, taking me to that nasty little diner, and then saying you had a headache and needed to go home—you're going to a hotel tonight with this Neanderthal? If the beer boy is what you want, then you can have him!" He turned and stalked out of the shop.

"Give it a minute," I said to Todd. "Wait until he gets out of sight."

When David was out of sight, Todd and I doubled over in a fit of laughter.

"I'm sorry," Todd said. "I couldn't help myself. You want me to tell him it was all a joke?"

"No," I said. "Besides, I really am going to the Grand Mountain Lodge tonight."

He raised his brows. "I'll get out my dancing shoes."

I laughed again. "I'm not planning on dancing." I explained my plan about talking with Caleb Santiago. "I want to ask him what he thought of Francesca Ortega and why he fired her. There's something that doesn't add up with that story."

"I agree. My assistant manager is off tonight, but I can—"

"Nonsense. I can handle this." I smiled. "You've already helped out more than you know."

"I'll tell David the truth if you want me to," Todd said.

"I don't want you to. I'm fed up with him. I can't believe I was actually going to marry that man at one point in my life. Do you know how miserable I'd be right now if I had?" I shook my head in disbelief. "But when he didn't show up for our wedding, I was heartbroken. He cannot possibly be the same guy I thought I was in love with."

"Maybe it's you. Maybe you're not the same girl."

"Either way, I'm glad he's gone," I said. "We're not right for each other."

"I'm glad." Todd searched my face with his warm brown eyes. "Maybe someday that trip to the Grand Mountain Lodge won't be so far-fetched."

"Maybe it won't."

"Be careful tonight, and call me if you need me," he said. "Santiago might not be willing to talk about his former employees with a stranger, and your audacity in asking might tick him off."

"That may be true, but I've got to try. And I'll be tactful." I shrugged. "Besides, the worst he can do is have Grand Mountain's security people throw me out, right?"

At around three o'clock that afternoon, I called Ted. I wanted to see if there had been any new developments in the case before I went to Toledo to talk with Mr. Santiago.

"Hi," I said when he answered his phone. "Do you have a second?"

"Always for you," he said.

"I know you aren't supposed to discuss this with me, so it's okay if you can't tell me anything. But have there been any new developments in the Francesca Ortega murder?"

He lowered his voice. "Her purse was found in

a Dumpster between Depoe Bay and Lincoln City early this morning. There were no prints on it."

"Not even Francesca's?" I asked.

"No. It was wiped clean." He paused. "I hear your brain cells buzzing. What are you up to?"

"Caleb Santiago Jr. will be at the Grand Mountain Lodge in Toledo later this afternoon," I said. "I'm going to try to talk with him."

"About what?" Ted asked. "There's nothing to tie him to Ms. Ortega's murder."

"But, like I've heard a certain law officer say over and over again, everyone's a suspect."

"Marcy, you can't just wander up to the man and ask him if he killed Francesca Ortega."

"I know that," I said. "I'll be subtle. I—we—have to find out where the jewels came from. Once we know that, we'll be able to find the killer. Don't you agree?"

"I do agree, but I don't like you veering off on your own and pretending to be Nancy Drew or Jessica Fletcher."

"I prefer Nancy. She's a little stuffy, but she's a lot younger than Jess."

"This isn't a joke," he said.

"I know. But don't you agree that I'm in a better position to ask off-the-wall questions of Mr. Santiago than you are?" I asked. "I can come across as a ditzy but concerned citizen who's afraid somebody out there thinks I still have some of the jewels Ms. Ortega brought me."

"Let me go with you," Ted said. "I'll wear plainclothes. He'll never peg me as a cop."

"I'd peg you as a cop if you were wearing your pajamas," I said. "Trust me. I can handle this."

"All right, but if you need me, call me."

"I will," I promised.

"And as soon as you talk with Santiago, call me and let me know what he said."

"Okay. Wish me luck."

"Marcy?"

"Yeah?"

"Be careful. Please." He sighed. "You're a magnet for mishap."

Chapter Ten

I closed up the shop shortly after talking with Ted and took Angus home. I fed him and then put him outside before bathing and changing clothes. I'd worn jeans to work today, but I wanted to wear something nicer to the Grand Mountain Lodge. I was guessing that the businessmen—including Mr. Santiago—would be wearing suits to the meeting. I had an adorable navy tweed suit with white ribbon accents that would be perfect for a business meeting. Sure, I realized I wouldn't be allowed into the meeting, but a girl has to look the part. Right?

Four-inch navy stilettos and a pencil skirt do not make for easy access into the Jeep. I thought for a moment I was going to have to get a block to step up on in order to get in. Finally, I was able to grab on to the steering wheel and pull myself up without ripping my skirt or getting a run in my hose. That was a major accomplishment.

I typed the Grand Mountain Lodge address into my GPS and headed for Toledo. I noticed a strange black sedan fall in behind me seconds after I left the driveway. I didn't think much of it until it began to take every turn I took. It made me uneasy. Still, it wasn't even four thirty in the afternoon yet. Who preys on a woman in broad—or, in this case, overcast, dusky, rather narrow—daylight? I shivered at the remembrance that Francesca Ortega had been stabbed outside my shop during the early-morning rush, and no one had admitted to seeing anything.

Hoping it was just a coincidence and that I was being paranoid, but keeping an eye on the car anyway, I drove on to the Grand Mountain Lodge. I pulled up to the front entrance where a valet rushed over to open the door for me.

"Good afternoon, ma'am," he said. "May I park your car for you?"

"Please," I said.

He took my hand and helped me out of the Jeep. That was worth a whopping tip right there. I thanked him, gave him the tip, and walked up to the door.

The doorman opened the door, and I took a quick glance over my shoulder before stepping into the warm interior of the hotel. The car that had been following me was nowhere in sight.

I looked around the lobby. The room was decorated in rich browns and wines. Gleaming leather sofas and overstuffed armchairs were grouped around a fireplace in the left corner. To my right was the registration desk. A young, thin man wearing a tan suit was currently manning the desk.

I walked over and gave him what I hoped was my most charming smile. "Hi, there. I'm looking for the meeting room."

"Which one?" he asked.

"For the Santiago Corporation."

He instructed me to go down the hallway and to my right.

I easily found the meeting room. I peeped inside and saw a long, glass-topped table surrounded by gray executive armchairs. A man and a woman were already in the room, and they appeared to be getting everything set up. The man was placing portfolios in front of the chairs, and the woman was pouring water into tumblers and setting those on the table.

"May I help you?" the man asked.

"I take it Caleb isn't here yet?" I asked.

"No, but he'll be down in a few minutes," he said. "Shall I tell him you're here?"

"Oh no," I said. "I wouldn't want to rush him."

"Would you like to come on in and sit down?" the woman asked.

"No, thank you. I've been driving and would

like to stretch my legs for a few minutes." With a smile, I turned and walked back up the hallway. If I hung around in this corridor, I was bound to meet up with Caleb Santiago.

I paced and watched for what seemed like an hour but was really more like fifteen minutes. Finally, my perseverance paid off. Caleb Santiago came rushing down the hall flanked by assistants. One assistant—a leggy blonde in a red suit—was on the phone. The other assistant was a man wearing gray pinstripes and talking with Santiago. It appeared he was trying to set out a game plan for the meeting.

"Excuse me, Mr. Santiago," I said. "I'm Marcy Singer. May I have a brief word with you?"

The male assistant looked annoyed and started to blow me off.

"Two minutes, Charlie," Mr. Santiago said, stepping over to me. "What can I do for you? Are you a reporter?"

"No, I'm not," I said. "Actually, I own the Seven-Year Stitch embroidery specialty shop, and I'd like to talk with you for just a few minutes—after your meeting, if possible—about Francesca Ortega."

Mr. Santiago started shaking his head.

"It's about the jewels she had in her possession," I blurted. "I'm afraid the man who killed her might come after me next."

He furrowed his brow. "We'll have dinner in

the dining room after my meeting and discuss it then."

"Great," I said. "Thank you. I'll wait for you at the bar."

He grinned. "Don't get too tipsy."

"I'll stick with soda," I promised. "Thanks again."

He nodded at me, then at his two assistants, and then he walked into the conference room.

I had to wonder if he was giving me the brush-off in a nice way and would "forget" to meet me after his conference, or if what I'd said about the jewels had struck a nerve.

I turned and had started to walk back down the hallway when I nearly bumped into another man heading for the meeting.

"Hi," he said, grinning and breathless. "Are you late for this thing, too?"

"No," I said. "I . . . I'm not invited."

"I wish I wasn't." He held out his hand. "Nicholas Santiago."

Of course. I should've recognized him from his photo on the Web site. I shook his hand. "Marcy Singer. It's nice to meet you."

"You, too. Hope to see you around." He winked and went into the conference room.

The younger brother seemed much more friendly and carefree than Caleb.

I headed for the bar and caught a glimpse of someone moving behind a large column.

Was I imagining things? Or was the person I'd suspected of following me earlier here at the lodge now? I thought about going around the column to confront the person, but I was afraid to. If this was the same man—or woman—who'd stabbed Francesca Ortega on the street outside my shop, he or she wouldn't hesitate to stab me here.

I went on into the bar. It wasn't terribly crowded yet, and I found a stool where I could be alone, see the door, and not be overheard. I ordered a Diet Coke from the bartender and took my phone from my purse.

"Ted Nash," he answered on the first ring.

"Ted, it's me."

"What's wrong?" he asked. "You sound scared."

I told him I suspected I had been followed to the lodge and how I thought someone was watching me here. "I'm probably being neurotic, but I just wanted to hear a friendly voice. And I wanted you to tell me what to do."

"Where are you now?"

"I'm in the bar drinking a Diet Coke. Caleb Santiago said he'd find me here after his meeting and that we could discuss Francesca Ortega over dinner." The bartender set my drink in front of me, and I mouthed a thank-you.

"So you aren't alone right now," Ted said.

"No. The bartender isn't two feet away."

"Stay there, then. I'm on my way."

"No, please. You don't have to come," I said.

"I'm probably being ridiculous, and I'll wind up dragging you away for nothing."

"Being assured of your safety isn't 'nothing.' I'll be there."

"But what about Santiago?" I asked.

"If you and he have dinner, I'll wait. I'm already in my car and on my way there, Marce."

I started to protest again, but I really wanted him to come. I was scared. "Thank you."

"You're welcome. Sit tight and I'll be there in less than half an hour."

"But it took me forty minutes to get here," I said.

"You weren't in a police car."

After we hung up, I sipped my soda, watched the door, and felt glad the cavalry was on its way. The bartender placed a bowl of pretzels in front of me, and I munched on those while I watched and waited . . . waited and watched.

Ted was correct in his assessment of how long it would take him to get to me. I spotted him coming through the door of the bar twenty-eight minutes after we'd hung up the phone. He hurried over to me.

"I didn't see anyone or anything suspicious-looking when I came through the lobby," he said. "But, to be honest, I was concentrating more on getting to you than on seeing who was out there. Are you okay?"

"I'm fine. Thanks for coming."

"You're welcome." He dug into my pretzels as the bartender came over. "Coke, please." He turned back to me. "I'll go back out into the lobby and walk around in a minute. Anything else weird happen?"

"No," I said. "Everyone who's come into the bar since I've been here was either with someone or joined someone." I bit my lower lip. "Do you think I overreacted?"

"Of course not. Always listen to your gut reaction."

The bartender brought Ted's drink. Ted thanked the man and then took a long drink.

"I'll be right back," he told me.

In a few minutes he was back to report that he hadn't seen anything out of the ordinary in the lobby and that he'd checked the bathrooms on the lower level. "Men's and women's."

My brows shot up. "I didn't hear any screams."

"I was discreet." He smiled.

I spotted Caleb Santiago coming into the bar. "That's him," I whispered. "That's Santiago."

"Have your meeting. I'll stay right here and keep an eye on both you and the door. When you leave, I'll follow you out," he said. "Don't worry. I won't let anything happen to you."

I got up off the bar stool and went to greet Mr. Santiago. "How was your meeting?"

"Productive. Thanks for asking," Mr. Santiago said. "So, are you ready for dinner?"

"I am."

Mr. Santiago nodded to the hostess, who rushed over and seated us at an intimate table in the corner. She introduced herself, gave us menus, and said our server would be right over.

"Won't your assistants or your brother be joining us?" I asked.

"Nope," he said with a grin. "It's just you and me. I spoke with my dad earlier. He said you're the one who told him about Francesca Ortega's murder."

"I am. I understood from Frederic, her son, that she'd worked with your father—and later, with you—for more than twenty years," I said. "I thought your dad would want to know about her death."

"That was nice of you."

The server arrived, introduced herself, and took our drink orders.

"What did you want to ask me about Ms. Ortega?" Mr. Santiago asked. "It must have been important to you for you to drive all the way here to talk with me."

"I don't mean to sound indelicate," I said. "I mean, I realize Ms. Ortega hasn't been dead a week even. But . . ."

"But?" he prompted.

"Was she a crook?"

Mr. Santiago looked stunned by my question, but before he could comment, the server arrived with our drinks—red wine for Mr. Santiago and water for me—and asked if we'd decided what we'd be having for dinner.

"Filet mignon medium well and baked potato for the both of us," Mr. Santiago said, "if that's all right with you, Ms. Singer."

"Sounds great," I said.

"All right," said the server. "I'll bring out your house salads with—"

"Bring them out when our food is ready," Mr. Santiago said. "We'd like a few minutes to talk undisturbed."

"Oh . . . okay, then." The server turned and scurried away from the table.

"Why do you ask if Ms. Ortega was a crook?" he asked me.

"After her death outside my shop, Frederic told me you'd fired her for snooping through your desk," I said.

"Go on."

"Let me back up a bit. Cassandra, Frederic's fiancée, wanted me to embellish a vintage wedding gown that had belonged to her mother. Ms. Ortega provided gems to go on this dress. I thought the gems were fake, and I think Cassandra and Frederic did, too."

"But they weren't?" Mr. Santiago asked.

"No. While investigating the murder, the police confiscated the gown and the gems in my possession and had them appraised. They were definitely not fake. In fact, the police believe the jewels given to me to adorn the dress were worth between seventy-five thousand and a hundred thousand dollars."

He whistled under his breath. "Ms. Ortega wasn't a wealthy woman. It embarrasses me to say so, but we didn't pay her well enough for her to afford gems like that."

"I knew she wasn't wealthy because Frederic said his mother would have to move in with him and Cassandra after the wedding," I said. "That's why my two main concerns are where Ms. Ortega got the jewels and whether or not her killer believes I still have some of them in my shop."

"Why do you think Ms. Ortega's murder and the gems are related? Couldn't it simply be a coincidence that she was killed while she had the stones with her?"

"I guess it's possible that it could've been a random mugging." I caught myself just before I said that whoever had killed Ms. Ortega had been a professional. I wasn't supposed to know that, and I didn't want to get Ted in trouble. I would have glanced in his direction, but I was facing away from the bar. "But that still doesn't answer the question of where Ms. Ortega got the stones in the first place."

"No, it doesn't." Mr. Santiago took a sip of his wine. "And you think she might have stolen them?"

"That's what I wanted to ask you," I said. "If

you did catch her snooping through your desk, then that proves she wasn't trustworthy, right?"

"I suppose that's true enough."

"It made you angry enough to fire her," I said. "Was that an isolated incident, or was it normal behavior that you simply refused to put up with anymore?"

He frowned. "I always got a bad vibe about Ms. Ortega. It wasn't something I could put my finger on, but it was definitely there. You know what I mean?"

"Of course. Were any of your clients jewelers?" I asked.

"Oh, I'm sure we have clients who own jewelry stores," he said. "We have so many it's hard to keep track, but there are bound to be a few. Wouldn't you think?"

"I'd think so, yes. And couldn't Ms. Ortega—for the sake of argument—have used information provided to your Web site to figure out how to rob the store?"

"She wasn't very adept at the computer. That's another reason for her dismissal. She failed to keep up with the times. But—as you said, for the sake of argument—I suppose she could have found what she needed to rob a store." He tilted his head. "Sure, it sounds pretty far-fetched, but I suppose it could've been done."

The server arrived with our food, asked if we needed drink refills, and then hurried off when we declined. Mr. Santiago had already intimidated her so badly she didn't want to linger.

"Maybe her son helped her," he said.

"Excuse me?" I asked. Sorry, but I was already interested in my steak at that point.

"Her son," he repeated. "Maybe he helped her steal the jewels."

"I suppose that's possible," I said. "If that's so, then the mugger—if the jewels were what he was looking for—might seek out Frederic instead of me." I smiled slightly. "Or maybe I should hang a sign in my shop window: 'No jewels here! Confiscated by police.' "

He chuckled. "That might work." He looked thoughtful as he cut into his steak. "Talk with Frederic. He could possibly have the answers you need."

We made small talk as we finished our dinner. When the server brought our tab, Mr. Santiago insisted on paying.

"But I'm the one who asked you to talk with me," I said.

"Ah, but I can write this off as a business expense. And I can use all the tax write-offs I can get." He smiled cordially. "I enjoyed dinner, Marcy. I hope we meet again sometime, and I wish you luck in finding out where Francesca Ortega came up with those jewels."

"Thank you."

"May I walk you out?" he asked.

"That isn't necessary. Thanks again for your time."

I left the bar and went into the ladies' room off the lobby. I hoped Ted was nearby. He was. I didn't know how nearby until he stuck his head into the bathroom.

"Ted! What're you doing?"

"Making sure this area is secure." He bent down and looked to make sure there were no feet in any of the stalls. "It appears to be all right. I'll be outside the door if you need me."

When I stepped back out into the lobby, Ted was there to take me by the arm. His gaze encompassed the entire room as he guided me toward the door.

"Give me your claim ticket, and I'll have the valets bring our cars around," he said softly. "I'll check the backseats to make sure they're clear, and then I'll follow you home."

"Okay." I shivered slightly in the night air. I watched Ted hand our claim tickets to the valets. He was so commanding, it was hard for me to take my eyes off him. And he'd come here and wasted his night off for me. How sweet was that?

There was a sudden movement to my left. I whipped my head around to see David storming up the steps toward me. Before I could react further, Ted sprang into action. He leapt between David and me, rammed David in the solar plexus with his forearm, and knocked him down.

As David was getting up, Ted pulled his gun. "Stay down, and show me your hands."

The valets, doorman, and several onlookers were standing there slack-jawed.

"It's all right," Ted said. "I'm a detective with the Tallulah Falls Police Department." With his left hand, he reached into his jacket pocket and produced his badge.

"*Um*, Ted," I said. "That's David Frist."

"I don't care who he is," Ted said. "He's under arrest for stalking."

"Wait," David began, sitting on the walk with his hands in the air. "I'm not stalking. I know this woman."

"That's true," I began. "He—"

"Did you or did you not follow Ms. Singer here this evening?" Ted asked.

"Isn't this out of your jurisdiction?" David asked.

"Yes, it is. But I'm still a duly licensed officer with the authority to enforce the law, and I'm willing to detain you until an officer of the Toledo police force arrives." He nodded at the doorman. "Will you please make the call, sir?"

"I already have. They're on their way," said the doorman.

"Good job." Ted nodded again in approval.

"Ted, it's okay," I said softly.

"What type of car were you driving this evening?" Ted asked David. "Was it a black sedan?

And you might as well tell me the truth because I will find out."

"Yeah," David said. "I exchanged my rental car so Marcy wouldn't know it was me."

"Then you admit to following her," Ted said.

David heaved a breath. "Yeah. So what? I wasn't going to hurt her. What's the big deal?"

"The big deal is that in the state of Oregon what you did—following Ms. Singer and causing her alarm—is stalking, a Class-A misdemeanor that holds a maximum of one year potential jail time."

"I didn't mean to cause her alarm. I meant to see who she was with and . . . and why." David glared at me. "I thought you were supposed to be here with beer boy, but I guess it was the sheriff's turn this evening. How'd beer boy take the news?"

"Shall I add harassment to your charges? Because I will if you don't shut up." Ted stepped in front of me, effectively blocking me from David's sight. "You will not speak to the victim."

"Victim?" David shouted.

"In fact, you have the right to remain silent," Ted said.

Before Ted could finish reciting David's rights, a Toledo police car arrived. Two uniformed officers got out of the patrol car. Ted holstered his gun and explained the situation. David quickly got to his feet. One officer spoke with David while the other took my statement. After talking with me, the officer conferred with his partner and then wrote David a citation. To say David was livid was an understatement. He started yelling obscenities at Ted and me, and the Toledo officers had to threaten to arrest him in order to make him calm down and leave the lodge.

"What happens now?" I asked Ted.

"He'll have to appear in court and explain to a judge just what he was doing."

"You don't think he'll get jail time, do you?"

"Nah," Ted said. "If he's a first-time offender, he'll get a slap on the wrist. He might get out of it altogether if he hires an attorney."

I nodded.

"Don't feel sorry for him. When you called me, you were terrified."

"That's true," I admitted.

Ted asked the valets to get our cars. Even though David had left the lodge, Ted still checked the backseats of both cars.

"Are you okay to drive?" he asked me.

"Yeah, I'm fine."

"All right. See you at your place."

Chapter Eleven

When we arrived back at my house, Ted pulled into the parking lot right behind me. Before I could get out of the Jeep, though, he hurried to my side.

"Stay put and let me check things out," he said. "I'll help you out of there in just a sec."

"I don't think David would be stupid enough to come here tonight. Not after what happened at the lodge."

"I'm not taking any chances where you're concerned."

Ted peered over the fence and spoke to Angus, who was barking furiously in the backyard. He shone a flashlight all around the back and the front of the house. Then he returned to the driver's side of the Jeep and held out his arms.

I gratefully slid into his arms, and he set me on the ground.

"Unlock the door, and then I'll go in ahead of you and check everything out inside," he said. "Stay close to me, okay?"

"I will." Even though I thought Ted was going a little overboard, I did as he asked me to. I stayed on his heels as he did a quick search of the house. When we popped into the bedroom, I took off my shoes.

"Hope you don't mind," I said.

"Not at all. Would you like to change clothes before we go back downstairs?"

I contemplated his face for a moment, trying to decide whether he was being flirtatious or serious. I couldn't read him.

"Do you mind?" I asked. "I can change while you're looking over the rest of the upstairs."

"Go ahead. If I finish before you do, would you like for me to go down and let Angus inside?"

"Sure." I smiled. "Thank you."

Ted stepped out of the bedroom and pulled the door closed behind him. I traded my suit for jeans and a fuzzy pink cowl-necked sweater.

When I joined Ted downstairs, he and Angus were playing tug-of-war with a rope toy.

"Would you like something to drink?" I asked.

"A bottle of water would be great."

"Are you hungry? Did you eat at the restaurant?"

"Oh yeah. I had a burger while you and Mr.

Santiago were scarfing those filets." He allowed Angus to win the tug match.

I grinned. "Don't make me feel bad about having steak while you were having a burger. I didn't even really get a choice." I went into the kitchen and got us each a bottle of water. "Not that I minded. The steak was great."

"What do you mean, you didn't get a choice? He just ordered for the both of you?"

"Yeah," I said. "I got the impression he's the kind of guy who's used to making decisions and having everyone else go along with them." I handed him his water.

"Like you with dinner tonight."

"Well, yeah. I mean, I wanted the information he had to offer, he made a good choice, and he made the decision so seamless that I never even thought to question it."

"He's good." He took the cap off the bottle and had a sip of the water.

"Yeah." I frowned as I sat down on the sofa beside him. "It kind of makes me wonder just how smooth he is. Is he smooth enough to get away with anything he wants?"

"Like ordering the killing of Francesca Ortega?" Ted asked.

"Maybe. It seems highly unlikely, though. I mean, what reason would he possibly have for doing that? He'd already gotten rid of the woman. He fired her."

"True. But fired employees are often vocal employees." He took another drink of his water before replacing the cap. "What did he say about Ms. Ortega?"

"Not much," I said. "He told me she wasn't very computer literate and that's one of the reasons he fired her. But he didn't put it past her to steal the jewels."

"Were the jewels stolen from the Santiagos?" Ted asked.

"No. Or, at least, he didn't say they were. I asked him if she might have access to jewelry stores his company serviced, and he said she probably did." I curled my legs up under me. "He seemed to think that if she did steal the gemstones, she couldn't have done it without help—probably from Frederic." I stifled a yawn.

"You look exhausted. I should go so you can rest."

"I'm all right. I just didn't get much sleep last night," I said.

"Why is that?"

"I had a lot on my mind." I told Ted about going out with David just to make sure I was doing the right thing in turning him away.

"He obviously doesn't take rejection well," Ted said.

"Well, that could partially be my fault. David came to the store earlier today to ask me for another date. Actually, he asked me where we were going as if we already had a date."

"Sounds like Mr. Santiago minus the charm."

"When I said I was going to Toledo to the Grand Mountain Lodge this evening," I continued, "David asked if I was going with Todd. Todd came in just as the question was asked."

"And Todd went with it. Obnoxiously, if I know Calloway."

I nodded. "I could've cleared up the misconception, but I didn't. I was hoping David would get in a huff and leave—which he did—and that would be the end of it . . . which it obviously wasn't."

"Do you think David is a threat to you?"

"No. I think he's angry, his ego is bruised, and he's not ready to take no for an answer yet. But I don't think he's dangerous." I cocked my head. "Do you?"

"I don't know. That's one of the reasons I took the precautions I did when I followed you home."

"And the other reason?" I asked.

"Ms. Ortega's killer is still out there. We have no leads, but I don't like the fact that she was murdered outside your shop."

"That makes two of us. Are you saying I'm no longer a suspect?"

"You know I can't say that," he said.

"What's with your new partner?" I asked. "She doesn't seem to like me much."

"She's a rookie I'm training, and she doesn't like anyone very much."

"She appears to like you fairly well."

"You think so?" he asked with a mischievous grin. "What gave you that impression?"

"Oh, I don't know. Maybe it was the way you and she were yukking it up with the his-and-her travel mugs when you were walking from MacKenzies' Mochas the other morning."

He scooted closer to me. "You're jealous."

"Not jealous. Only curious." I glanced at him from the corner of my eye. "She is pretty."

"I guess," he said, still grinning. "If you go in for that type."

"Is she married?"

"No." He laughed. "You *are* jealous."

"I repeat: I'm not jealous. Only curious." I rested my head against the back of the sofa.

"Since we're confessing—sort of—I'll admit that I was fairly curious about David Frist Thursday morning when he said he was your fiancé in order to get into the shop," Ted said. "It felt good to take him down tonight."

"He's gonna be so mad at me," I said.

"If he comes around bothering you, call me," Ted instructed.

I nodded. I could feel my eyes drifting closed.

"Lie back and put your feet in my lap," he said.

"No, I'm fine."

He got up, eased me against the arm of the sofa,

and sat back down. He lifted my legs onto his lap. He gently took one foot in his hands and began massaging it.

I sighed. "That feels . . . so . . . good."

When I opened my eyes, the room was dark and I'd been covered by a soft green fleece blanket. The light in the living room had been turned off, but the light in the foyer had been left on to provide me sufficient light to see to go to bed. I sat up and stretched my arms up over my head. I stood and noticed that the clock read twelve forty-five a.m. It was a good thing I didn't have to go to work in the morning. Lying on the floor beside the sofa, Angus snuffled and changed positions.

I walked slowly from the living room into the foyer and saw a note on the table near the door.

> Hi:
>
> I locked the door behind me. Found the blanket in the hall closet. Hope you don't mind. I'll call you tomorrow.
>
> —Ted

I smiled slightly. The last thing I remembered before I dozed off was him rubbing my feet. What a special man.

I turned off the foyer light and went on upstairs. I slipped off my clothes and got into bed. I dreamed I was in a science lab with Caleb Santiago, who was wearing a white lab coat.

"I need a clone," I told him. "Can you do that for me?"

"You want a clone of what?" he asked. "We've cloned hard drives, of course. But if you're talking mammals, you may choose from a sheep, a rat, a mule, a monkey, or maybe a rabbit."

"No, no," I said. "I want you to clone *me*."

"What on earth for?"

"Because I can't choose between Todd and Ted. I care for them both." I began to cry.

"Sometimes decisions are hard to make," Mr. Santiago said. "Take my dad, for example. He liked Francesca Ortega. She'd been a loyal employee for years." He smiled. "But she wasn't family. He had a difficult choice to make, too, but he made the right one."

"Yes, but you said Francesca didn't keep up with the times and that she wasn't trustworthy."

"I did say that, didn't I? Where do you think she got those pretty gemstones?"

"I don't know," I said. "Do you?"

He gave me another enigmatic smile. "Of course I do."

"Where?" I leaned closer to hear where Francesca had gotten the jewels.

"On eBay," he whispered. And then he pressed his cold, wet nose to my forehead.

I jerked awake. "Angus! You scared the daylights out of me."

Angus, tail wagging, leapt onto the bed and back down again. He raced down the hall, ran back, and jumped back onto the bed. Once again, he tried to put his face in mine.

I pushed him away, yawned, and looked at the clock. It was seven thirty. He needed to go out. I quickly got out of bed and slipped on the jeans and sweater I'd been wearing last night.

"Let's go." Angus hurried down the stairs ahead of me and went straight to the back door.

I opened the door, and he rushed outside. As I made coffee, I wondered about the dream. It wasn't hard to interpret the cloning part of the dream. I really did care for both Ted and Todd. I knew that eventually I'd have to choose between them, but right now I simply couldn't. But as for the latter part of the dream, had Caleb Santiago done or said something that had made me believe—subconsciously—that he knew more about the jewels than he was indicating?

Sadie called while I was finishing my breakfast. Someone who knew someone who'd heard about the fiasco at Grand Mountain Lodge came into the café and was telling Sadie and Blake all about it. Of course, in their version, David had put a knife to my throat and was threatening to kill me and then himself. Ted had intervened—taking a vicious stab to the shoulder in the process—and had managed to wrestle the knife away from David.

I laughed. "That's much more exciting than what actually happened." I relayed to her the actual course of events.

"Oh," she said, sounding a little deflated. "The version I heard was better. Still, yours isn't bad. I'm glad Ted came to your rescue."

"So am I. I wish David hadn't been cited for stalking, though. He's going to be furious with me over that."

"Why should he be furious at you?" Sadie asked. "He admitted he'd changed rental cars to throw you off and that he followed you to the lodge. It's his own fault he got cited."

"Yeah, well, David doesn't accept blame graciously. I'm sure he'll think I blew everything out of proportion and made him pay the price for it."

"Do you think he'll retaliate?"

"In what way?"

"In any way," Sadie said. "You don't think he'll come after you, do you?"

"I wouldn't be surprised to get an angry phone call from him today, but maybe he'll take this as his cue to return to San Francisco."

"I hope so. You know Blake and I are here if you need us."

"Thanks," I said.

No sooner had Sadie and I finished our conversation than my doorbell rang. Angus was still outside romping in the backyard.

I went to the front door and wasn't terribly surprised to see David standing there.

"Are you alone?" he asked.

"Yes."

"May I come in?" He didn't seem as angry as I'd feared he'd be.

I stepped back from the door and allowed David into the foyer. I knew he'd been angry, but I couldn't really make myself believe I had anything to fear from him. "Would you like to talk in the living room?"

He nodded.

We went into the living room. The green blanket Ted had draped over me last night was still on the sofa. I picked it up and folded it before placing it on the ottoman. David sat on the chair, and I perched on the edge of the sofa.

"Last night was stupid," he said. "That guy made me crazy—acting like you and he were having some kind of romantic getaway at a fancy hotel. And then when you walked out with the cop . . ." He shook his head. "I lost it."

"David, I called Ted—the cop—because you frightened me by following me to the lodge. Didn't it cross your mind that I might be freaked out since a woman was stabbed outside my shop earlier in the week?"

He opened his mouth, closed it again, and looked thoughtful. "No, actually, that thought never occurred to me."

"If you hadn't started flinging accusations about my plans when you first came into the shop yesterday—and if Todd hadn't overheard you slamming him—I could've explained that I went to the lodge to try to get information on Ms. Ortega, the stabbing victim."

"Why?" he asked. "Why would you want information on her? She's dead, for goodness' sake. There's nothing you can do for her now."

"I realize that," I said. "But the person who killed her might be aware that she'd given me some of those gemstones to put on Cassandra's gown, and they might think I still have some."

"So you're afraid the killer will come after you?"

"Yeah," I said. "And until the police make an arrest and are sure they have the right person off the street, I'll have that fear."

David got up and came over to the couch. "Then let's go to the police department in Toledo and have those stupid charges against me dropped so we can go home to San Francisco."

"My life is here."

"Your death might be here, too. Come on, Marcy, *think*. We'll leave Tallulah Falls and open a shop in California. We'll sell the embroidery stuff . . . and maybe some art supplies. I used to sketch in college. Maybe I could take it up again . . . or do some painting. It'll be fun."

"What about the shop here?" I asked. "And my house?"

"Somebody will lease the shop," he said. "The woman who runs the aromatherapy shop said she had a sister just dying to open up an antique store. She said she'd intended to lease the building you're in, but you snapped it up first." He shrugged. "As for the house, maybe we can keep it as a summer home."

"Do you think I'm independently wealthy or something?"

"No, but your mom will help us."

I stood. "David, there is no us. Despite all of the other giant holes in your plan that you seem to be avoiding, that's the biggest one of all."

"There could be an us." He rose off the sofa and took my hands. "You just need to get away from all these distractions and give us a fighting chance. We were great together once. We could be again."

"We're different people now."

"How long are you planning to punish me for getting cold feet on our wedding day?" he asked. "I'm sorry. I wasn't ready then. I'm ready now."

"You're not the only one who has a horse in this race, David. It's not all about you."

He sighed. "You need to put this stabbing behind you. I get that. But maybe we can get these bogus charges against me dismissed and go from there."

He leaned in to kiss me, but I turned my head so that his lips landed on my cheek.

"Good-bye," I said.

He dropped my hands. "I'm not leaving Oregon. Not until I've brought you around to my way of thinking."

As he left, I thought, *David might be in Tallulah Falls for a lo-o-o-ong time.*

Chapter Twelve

Vera called around ten a.m. and asked me to go with her to Lincoln City to the costume shop where she'd seen the "perfect dress" for me to wear to the masquerade ball. And she wanted me to help her find her "perfect dress." I agreed to go, got ready, and placed Angus outside with his food, water, and favorite toys.

"I know I've been leaving you out here quite a bit lately," I told him as I held his face in my hands and looked into his dark eyes. "But I'll make it up to you when I get home. I promise. We'll have a movie and popcorn night—just you and me."

He looked skeptical, but I heard Vera's silver BMW pull up, and I didn't have time to further convince him. I hugged him, rushed back inside, locked the door, sped through the hallway, grabbed my purse off the table in the foyer, and went out the front door.

"Good morning," Vera said cheerily as I got into the car. "Can you believe it? Sunshine and warm weather—for us, in February!"

"I know. I didn't even need a heavy coat today." I held out the hem of my jean jacket. "It's gorgeous out."

Vera chattered on about the weather and how we should enjoy it while it lasted because that darn groundhog had seen his shadow the other day. Then she talked about the upcoming Valentine's Day, the masquerade ball, her latest cross-stitch project, and the friends she'd made while attending one of my needlework classes.

Mainly, I just listened. That's the good thing about Vera. She's more than willing to keep up both sides of a conversation if necessary. And I didn't have a whole lot to say this morning. Besides, I had to be careful about what information I chose to impart to Vera, because—as I've already indicated—Vera loves to talk. That's great unless she's talking about something you'd rather she didn't.

When we arrived at the dress shop in Lincoln City, she could hardly wait to show me the black and maroon ball gown. And I could hardly wait to see it. That is, until I saw it.

It was not what I'd imagined or hoped it would be. The dress was pretty—it had a black and maroon print bodice and underskirt with a black velvet overskirt—but it wasn't a dress I could imagine myself wearing to the masquerade ball. It was bulky and wide and heavy.

"Try it on," Vera said, smiling broadly.

Not wanting to disappoint her, I tried on the dress. Luckily for me, it was much too large and was the only one they had of its kind, so I didn't have to make excuses for not buying the dress.

"I'm so sorry," Vera said. "Don't you think we could alter it in time for the ball, though? You're quite handy with a needle."

"I'm afraid I'm not that great with alterations," I said. "I'm sure my mom could've made the dress work had she been here, but unfortunately she's in New York." And then I spotted it. The dress that made me draw in my breath. "But look, Vera. Look at that one."

Vera and the saleswoman followed me through the store to where a white beaded gown was hanging.

"May I try on this one?" I asked the saleswoman.

"Of course," she said. Once again, she led me to the fitting room.

I tried on the dress, and it fit like it had been made for me. The gown had narrow straps, a straight, tight-fitting bodice, and a skirt that flowed into a slight train. I ran my hands lightly down the beaded skirt. Oh yeah, this was definitely it.

I stepped out of the fitting room. "What do you think?"

"It's lovely," said the saleswoman, clasping her hands together. "You'll be the belle of the ball for certain in that dress."

"It looks too much like a wedding gown," Vera complained, her heart still on the maroon and black gown. "It doesn't seem festive enough for a masquerade ball."

"Oh, I think it does. I think it's pure understated elegance." The saleswoman retrieved a white beaded and feathered mask that matched the gown perfectly. "Here. Put this on, dear, and let's see how they look together."

I added the mask and smiled at myself in the mirror. "I'll take it."

Although still rather put out that I didn't go with the gown she'd chosen, Vera perked up after we found her a gold brocade gown with a black lace inset at the bodice and a full skirt that required a petticoat with a hoop. She bought a black and gold mask to go with the dress and said she'd feel just like a queen at the ball. I assured her she'd look the part.

Once we'd bought our gowns, we went to a nearby café for lunch. It wasn't MacKenzies' Mochas, but it was still good. Vera and I both ordered chef's salads and water.

While we were eating, she asked me if the police had any leads on who'd killed Francesca Ortega.

"I don't think so," I said.

"Poor woman. That's a shame. It makes you wonder what the world is coming to." Vera shook her head sadly. "You know that robber could've taken her purse without killing her."

"Yeah, I know." I speared a cherry tomato with my fork. "Her son said Francesca used to work for the Santiago Corporation. Have you ever heard of them?" If anyone in Tallulah Falls would have any information about the Santiago Corporation, I figured Vera would. She tries to find out as much as possible about everyone and everything in town, and her late husband used to be in banking.

"Santiago Corporation." Vera frowned. "No, I can't say I've heard of them. Do they have an office near Tallulah Falls?"

"Not yet, but I believe they're getting ready to open a branch in Toledo."

"Oh yeah," she said. "I saw that Caleb Santiago in the newspaper the other day. Maybe he'll come to the masquerade ball. He's a nice-looking young man."

Instead of commenting, I had a bite of salad.

"Not that you need any more young men falling at your feet." Vera giggled. "With Todd Calloway, Ted Nash, and that new one that's recently come calling, you have your hands full juggling dates. Have you decided on an escort for the masquerade ball yet?"

"Nope. No one has asked me. I might be going alone. Of course, that would certainly beat going with David—the new one who is actually an old one that I wish would go away again." I gave Vera an abbreviated version of the history between David and me.

"And now he thinks he can waltz right back into your life and pick up where he left off?" she asked. "He's got a lot of nerve."

"You're telling me. This morning he even suggested that we leave Tallulah Falls and open up a shop in California."

She held her fork halfway to her mouth. "Is he crazy? I mean, seriously, he could have some sort of mental problems."

"That could explain things," I said. "Get this. He said I wouldn't have trouble leasing the shop because Nellie Davis's sister has wanted it all along."

"Oh, good grief! Nobody cares about Hattie Davis and her old antique shop. Those are just two troublemaking biddies, and that David fellow needs to hit the bricks and keep on bouncing until he gets back to where he came from."

"I agree wholeheartedly." I raised my water glass in a toast. "Here's to David bouncing on home."

Vera touched her glass to mine. "And staying there."

After I got home, I put my dress and mask in my bedroom closet after making sure I had the perfect pair of strappy white sandals to complete the outfit. Buying the gown had me actually looking forward to the ball, even if I did end up going alone.

I went downstairs and let Angus into the house. He bounded in, happy and excited.

"I remember the promise I made to you this morning," I told him, hugging his thick neck. "Just you and me for movies and popcorn this evening. But first, I have to make a couple phone calls."

I gave him a bone that was supposed to clean his teeth and freshen his breath, while I curled up on the chair in the living room with my cell phone. It was a little chilly, so I got the blanket Ted had covered me with last night and placed it across my lap. I smoothed the fleece, thinking about how sweet he'd been to take such good care of me.

I called Ted first to thank him again, but my call went straight to voice mail. Suddenly I felt awkward about leaving a message and didn't know what to say, so I ended the call. Naturally, he'd see my number and realize he'd missed a call from me. Hoping he wouldn't think anything was wrong, I started to call him back. But then, that seemed pushy or desperate or something that I definitely was not. So I just let the whole matter go and called Riley.

"Hi," I said when she answered. "Is this a good time to talk?"

"I'm on bed rest," she reminded me. "Is there a bad time to talk?"

"Well, I thought you might be sleeping or being pampered by Keith."

"Nah, when I'm sleeping I turn my phone off. And I finally convinced Keith to go play basketball at the gym with some of his buddies. His fussing over me is precious, but it can get a little suffocating. Is it wrong to say I'm ready to have this baby already?"

"Of course it isn't. But you can't rush perfection, you know."

She laughed. "I know. I'm just so ready to have her here, to hold her, to get up and walk around again."

"I realize it's hard, but try to enjoy the bed rest while you can. From what I hear, there's no rest whatsoever for something like the first six years of your child's life," I said. "Or is it the first eighteen?"

"Oh, thank you, Marcy. That's ever so encouraging."

"Oops," I said with a laugh. "I was just trying to point out the silver lining to the bed rest. Is your mom holding down the fort at work?" Riley's mom was her administrative assistant.

"Yeah. I keep asking her to bring me work, but she doesn't want to. I tell her it'll give me something to do. I can be on bed rest and work very well on a laptop, you know." She sighed. "But enough about me. Did you meet with Santiago?"

"I did." I told Riley all about our dinner meeting and how Mr. Santiago seemed to think Francesca might've stolen the gemstones with help from her son. "I'm going to call Frederic and ask him to come to the shop tomorrow . . . without Cassandra."

"You're going to ask him if he helped his mother steal jewels the day before he buries her?" Riley asked incredulously.

"Not in so many words," I said. "Do you think my timing is off, that I should wait to talk with him?"

She was quiet for a moment, and I knew she was weighing the pros and cons. "No. Go ahead and call him. See if there's anything he needs—any way you can help him prepare for Tuesday. And then when you get him alone at the shop, act like you think Santiago is trying to set him up."

"What?"

"Trust me," she said. "It's an excellent strategy for getting a witness to cooperate. Make him believe you're on his side, that you think he and his mother are innocent. Show him you're his ally. Let him take you into his confidence."

"Okay. It seems kinda sneaky, but who knows? That might be what's happening, after all. We don't know," I said. "Frederic did work for the corporation, too. Maybe he and Caleb Jr. didn't get along. At least it'll be a way to get Frederic to open up to me more . . . hopefully."

"Great. Let me know what you find out."

"I will," I said. "By the way, did you learn anything in your online research about the Santiago Corporation that I should know?"

"I found out they had a lot fewer hassles and lawsuits and seemed to run a cleaner operation all around while Mr. Santiago Sr. was at the helm. Since Junior has taken over, there have been a lot of questions—so far unsubstantiated, but questions nonetheless—about the company's business dealings."

"Thanks, Riley."

After talking with Riley, I called Frederic Ortega. Like Ted's, Frederic's call went straight to voice mail. Unlike with Ted's, I left Frederic a message. I asked him to either call me back this evening or come by the Seven-Year Stitch tomorrow. I indicated there was something I wanted to speak with him about. I didn't specify that he shouldn't bring Cassandra, but I didn't say I wanted to speak with him and Cassandra. I hoped he'd read between the lines on that one.

Last, but not least, I called Todd.

"Hey, there," he said. "I was just thinking of calling you. How'd it go last night?"

"It was . . . interesting." I filled Todd in on Caleb Santiago's belief that Francesca and Frederic might've stolen the jewels.

"I've been thinking about those jewels," Todd said. "You said you thought they were fake beads when you first got a look at them, right?"

"That's right, I did."

"Then they must have been part of a matched set," he said. "You know, like a necklace or bracelet where each stone is cut and polished to match the others."

"Of course." I sat up straighter. "Or they could've come from several pieces of jewelry that had been dismantled in order to sell the stones."

"Exactly. I've got a friend in the FBI. His field office is near Depoe Bay, and he owes me a favor. How about I ask him come by the Brew Crew tomorrow evening to talk with you about those stones, see if they match anything in the FBI's database of stolen jewelry?"

"That'd be great, Todd! Do you think he'll do it?"

"Yeah, I think he will if he's in town and doesn't have other plans. If he's able to come, I'll have him call you in the morning at the shop so you can tell him all about the jewels. That way, he'll have an idea of what he's looking for before he meets with you tomorrow evening," Todd said. "I'll call him now and see what I can arrange."

"Thank you. I appreciate your help. Oh, and by the way . . ." I went on to tell Todd about David following me to the lodge because he thought Todd and I were having a rendezvous.

"Why would he have to follow you to find that out?" Todd asked. "I told him we were."

"I don't know. Actually, this morning, he told me the thought of us going to the lodge together made him crazy," I said.

"This morning?" Todd's voice turned cool.

"Yeah. Ted having him cited for stalking last night didn't go over well, and he came by this morning to ask me to drop the charges."

"Nash had him arrested?" Todd asked, with an incredulous laugh.

"Not quite arrested." I explained the events leading up to and including the takedown where Ted actually pushed me behind him and shoved David to the ground.

"Had it been me, I'd have punched the guy," he said. "But you did the right thing in calling Nash. If you think your life may be in danger, then he's probably your go-to guy."

There was a note of disappointment in Todd's voice, and I wished I hadn't mentioned David or Ted. I thought Todd would find it amusing that our fabricated passionate plans led to David getting a stalking citation, but I didn't want it to appear I'd chosen Ted over him. Of course, I had . . . in this case . . . but Ted is a law enforcement officer. Todd was right: Ted's my go-to guy in a life-and-death situation. But what about other situations? Who was my overall go-to guy? I didn't have an answer for that.

Angus returned with the remnants of his breath-freshening bone and sprawled out at my feet.

Well, there you go, I thought. Angus is my overall go-to guy . . . at least for now.

I bent down and kissed his scruffy head. "Let's go for a run on the beach before we settle in for our movie night. What do you say?"

He woofed his agreement.

Chapter Thirteen

Vera had been right about the weather. Monday morning when Angus and I drove to the shop, we had the heater blasting and the windshield wipers on high.

"Rainy days and Mondays always get us down, don't they, Angus?" I asked.

He was too depressed to even answer. He simply sighed and slumped in his seat.

Upon arriving at the shop, I saw that Frederic Ortega was there ahead of us. He was standing on the sidewalk with an umbrella, and he was shivering. The Seven-Year Stitch opened at ten a.m. It was nine forty-five. I admire promptness, but after what happened to his mother, you'd think Frederic would've waited until at least ten thirty to come by.

I parked, and Angus and I got out of the Jeep and raced to the door.

"Good morning," I said to Frederic as I unlocked the door. I felt I should apologize to him for being late, even though I wasn't. I settled for "Sorry you had to wait." I turned on the lights.

"No problem," he said, closing the umbrella and placing it in the stand near the door. "I've only been here a couple minutes. I got your message."

Angus shook himself, raining droplets over everything within a two-yard radius, including Frederic and me. He then went to lie on his bed beneath the counter.

"Sorry about that," I said, depositing my purse and the tote bag with the Kuba cloth quilt project behind the counter. "Would you like some coffee or tea?"

"No, thank you. I'm fine." He slipped off his damp coat.

"May I put that in the office for you?"

"Please." He handed me his coat, and I hung both our coats on a rack in my office.

I returned to find him sitting in one of the sit-and-stitch chairs looking contemplative. "Penny?"

He frowned. "Excuse me?"

"You know, for your thoughts. A penny for your thoughts?"

"Oh yes, of course." He rubbed his forehead. "I dread tomorrow."

"I'm sure you do. That's one of the reasons I asked you to come by. I wanted to ask if there's anything you and Cassandra need . . . anything I can do for you."

He lowered his hand and looked pleasantly surprised. "You sound sincere. I think you really mean that."

"I do mean that," I said. "I didn't know your mother really—and I don't know you and Cassandra well, either, for that matter—but I understand what you must be going through. I lost my father when I was young. Is there some way I could help?" I sat down on the sofa that faced away from the window. "I could document who sent flowers to the funeral home and prepare thank-you cards for your signature. I can address the envelopes, too, and then all you'll have to do is sign the cards, put stamps on them, and mail them."

"You would do that for me?" He shook his head. "Really?"

"Of course. Would that help?"

His face crumpled, and he began to cry. I handed him the tissue box.

Oh, crap. I'm a jerk. I'm worse than a jerk. . . . I'm a jerk who's trying to get a guy whose mother just died to implicate himself in a jewel theft.

"I'm so sorry," I said to Frederic.

The bells over the shop door jingled, and I turned to see who'd come in. It was Ted and the rookie, Harriet Sloan. I went over to them.

"Is this a bad time?" Ted asked.

"His mother's funeral is tomorrow," I whispered.

"I need to speak with you in private, Ms. Singer," Ted said. "Detective Sloan, would you please keep Mr. Ortega company while Ms. Singer and I confer in her office?"

"Of course." With barely a glance in my direction, Detective Sloan hurried to Frederic's chair, where she stooped down and began talking to him in a soothing voice.

Ted followed me into my office and closed the door.

"What is it?" I asked. "What's wrong?"

He immediately took me in his arms. "I had to see you and make sure you're all right."

He was holding me a little too tight, but it was nice. I looked up into his eyes. "I'm fine."

My gaze dropped to his full lips. I knew that if I gave him just the slightest invitation, he'd kiss me right now. And part of me wanted that. Part of me wanted that pretty badly. But the other part of me was hearing the disappointment in Todd's voice last night after I told him I'd called Ted to come to my rescue.

I dragged my eyes away from his lips. He was saying something, and I'd missed most of it. "What's that?"

"I'm sorry I didn't return your call last night," he said huskily. "The battery on my phone died. I charged it, but I didn't see that you'd called until—"

I gently moved out of his embrace. "It's all right." I smiled. "If that's the reception I get when you don't return a call, then don't return my calls."

"Did that creep bother you yesterday?"

"Not really. He came by and asked me to drop the charges and to give him a fighting chance."

Ted clenched his jaw. "I'll give him a fighting chance."

"You already have," I said. "You didn't shoot him. Besides, I sent him away, and he went. He was pretty docile about it, too, come to think of it."

"He'd better be if he values his health."

I smiled again. "Thank you." The sparks flying between us were about to catch my office on fire. "We really should get back out there."

I averted my eyes, stepped around Ted, and opened the door. Instead of going straight into the shop, I darted into the bathroom and held a cold, wet paper towel on the back of my neck until my heartbeat returned to within about fifty beats of normal.

When I stepped into the shop, I saw that Harriet Sloan and Frederic were still talking. They had their bowed heads together. Suddenly Harriet Sloan said, "Amen."

Great. While I was contemplating giving in to my lust for Ted in my office, Harriet was out here praying with Frederic.

"Ms. Singer," Ted said, "I'll definitely be following up with you later."

"Please do," I said. I could be sassy, too.

"And, Frederic, I'll check on you later today," Detective Sloan said. "If you need me, you have my number."

Ted and Detective Sloan left. I returned to the sofa.

"Are you okay?" I asked Frederic.

He nodded. "Harriet is a special girl. And so are you. I appreciate your help. I only wish . . ."

"You only wish what?" I prompted.

"I only wish Cass would be half as supportive as either of you." He raised his eyes to mine. "I love Cass—or, at least, I thought I did—but now I don't think we're right for each other. Our priorities aren't the same."

"It's better to come to that realization before the wedding than after." After our colossal failure of a date Friday night, I knew now that David not showing up for our wedding was the kindest thing he could've done for me. Had I married him, I either would not have grown into the woman I was today, or would have eventually, and then I would have been miserable with David. "Trust me. I know what I'm talking about."

"Yeah, I suppose you're right," Frederic said. "Before I forget, there's something that's been troubling me. That man who was here the other morning—Thursday morning—he looked familiar to me. What's his name?"

"David Frist."

Frederic's eyes narrowed. "David Frist. What was he doing here?"

"Funny you should ask." I gave an awkward chuckle. "David was my equivalent to your Cassandra. Even though he was the one who decided we weren't right for each other on the day of our wedding well over a year ago, I'm the one who's now realizing he made the best possible decision for both of us."

"I was too distraught to pay much attention to him when I first saw him, but now I have to wonder why an employee of the Santiago Corporation was here in your shop on the morning my mother was killed on your sidewalk."

"You must have David confused with someone else," I said, frowning. "He's currently out of work."

"Maybe so, but he used to have a fairly high-ranking position at the Santiago Corp. working directly with Caleb Jr."

"David? David Frist?" I asked. "Are you sure?"

Frederic shrugged. "If you don't believe me, ask him."

"I will. Not because I don't believe you, but because that's a heck of a coincidence, don't you think?"

"Oh yeah. I do think that . . . if it is, in fact, a coincidence."

I leaned forward. "Frederic, we have to find out

who murdered your mother." I told Frederic about meeting with Caleb Santiago on Saturday.

"What were you doing poking into the Santiago Corporation's—and my mother's—business?" he asked.

"When I realized that whoever killed her might think I still have the jewels she brought here, I got scared. I thought Mr. Santiago might be able to tell me something that would lead police to the killer."

"I guess you've got a point," he said. "What did Junior have to say for himself?"

I bit my lower lip. "He was probably just trying to throw me off track, but . . . he led me to believe that you and your mother might've stolen the jewels."

"He *what*?" Frederic stood and clenched his fists. "He'll pay for this."

I stood and took Frederic's arm. "I believe he could be trying to set you up."

Frederic sat back down, and so did I.

"We need to work together," I said. "Do you have any idea where your mother got those gemstones?"

"No. I thought they were costume jewelry . . . that she'd bought them at a craft store or something. I don't know. I certainly didn't think they were real jewels. She probably didn't think they were real, either."

I somehow doubted that. I debated on whether

or not I should tell Frederic I might be meeting with an FBI agent this evening, but I decided against it. I needed Frederic's help, but I couldn't forget that he might be playing me—that he really might have had something to do with where his mother got the jewels. I didn't think he had anything to do with her death, but I didn't know Frederic well enough to trust him completely.

"But her killer knew the jewels were real," I said. "Or, at least, I think he did."

"I think he did, too." Frederic cocked his head. "So, what do we do next?"

"First off, don't confront Caleb Santiago. He can't know you and I have discussed him or the jewels. If he does, he'll never confide anything to either of us. You also need to try to find out where your mother got those gemstones. Look through her things and see what you can come up with."

"I'll do that. In fact, I'll go do that now," he said.

"I'll get your coat." I went to the office and got Frederic's coat. "By the way, I'm serious about those thank-you cards."

Frederic took his coat from me and put it on. "I appreciate that, but Harriet said she'll collect the cards off the flower arrangements at the funeral home. She and I are going to go through them later today to see if any names jump out at me."

"Why?" I asked. "Does she think someone connected with your mother's death would actually send flowers to the funeral home?"

"She said it's a strong possibility. The guilty person might send flowers to make himself appear innocent." He retrieved his umbrella. "I'll let you know if I come across anything suspicious. In the meantime, be leery of David Frist."

"Believe me, I will."

Frederic left, and I strode into my office and turned on my computer. I heated up some water in the microwave and made myself an instant cappuccino while the computer was booting up. Then I e-mailed Riley.

I explained to Riley in the message that I'd spoken with Frederic.

> During our conversation, he asked David's name—he told me David looked familiar to him the other morning but that he was too distraught to give it much thought. When I told him David's name, he told me David works at the Santiago Corporation! Could you please check into this for me?

I then filled Riley in on my possible meeting with the FBI agent Todd knew, told her I hoped she was feeling well, and asked her to call me if she needed anything or when she found something out about David.

> I intend to ask him about it, but I'm not sure he'll give me a straight answer.

As I sent the e-mail, I wondered about what Frederic had said. He'd recognized David, and then when I told him David's name, he'd recognized that, too. David told me he was out of work. He did say he'd been from one job to another, so maybe he had worked for Santiago sometime in the past.

While I was online, I ordered some spring-themed cross-stitch and needlepoint kits. I also ordered enough yarn, embroidery threads, and perle flosses to replenish my stock. Then I went into the sit-and-stitch square and worked on the Kuba cloth quilt. I almost had it finished.

Vera came in close to lunchtime. She sat on the sofa across from me and smiled at me expectantly.

"I don't know why," I admitted, "but that look on your face is making me nervous."

"I want you to make me a purse to match my dress," she said.

"I'm flattered you have such a high opinion of my abilities," I said, "but—"

"You're welcome," she interrupted, taking a piece of paper from her purse and handing it to me. "I want it to be gold, like my dress. Or you could make the purse black, if you'd like, and adorn it with gold satin roses."

I unfolded the paper and looked at it. It looked easier than I'd thought it would. The purse like the one Vera wanted me to make her was covered in large satin ribbon embroidery roses.

"I can do this," I said.

Vera clasped her hands together. "I knew you could!"

I did a mental inventory to see if I had everything on hand to make the purse. I had the satin ribbon, and I had a tapestry needle with an eye large enough to accommodate the ribbon, but I didn't have any plain black or gold fabric or a chain handle for the purse. I mentioned that fact to Vera.

"Tell me what you need," she said. "I'll get it for you and bring it to you in the morning."

I smiled. Her excitement was contagious. "All right."

I went to the counter, took out a notepad, and made a list of the additional items Vera would need in order for me to complete the purse.

She left, happily anticipating a purse to match her ball gown.

My mind turned back to David. From my phone, I checked my e-mail. There wasn't a follow-up message from Riley yet. I hoped everything was okay. And I hoped Frederic Ortega was mistaken in his belief that David had worked for the Santiago Corporation.

Chapter Fourteen

The FBI agent Todd had spoken with me about called around two p.m. He told me he'd talked with Todd about the gems and the stabbing, and he asked me to describe the stones I'd seen. I did so. He said he'd take a look at the FBI stolen-jewelry database and that he'd meet me at around six this evening at the Brew Crew.

Just after we'd spoken, a vase of salmon-colored roses was delivered to me by the local florist. I opened the card with dread, expecting the flowers to be from David. I was pleasantly surprised. The card read:

> These match the color of your lipstick. I know because I was staring at your mouth pretty intently this morning. Will you go

with me to the masquerade ball on Saturday?

—Ted

I smiled to myself. I also blushed. I could picture him at the florist's boutique looking for roses that would match my lipstick. And the funny thing was, they really did match perfectly!

Once again, I found myself thrown into a dilemma about choosing between Ted and Todd. But Todd hadn't asked me to the ball, and Ted just had. Of course, I'd go to the ball with Ted. Besides, it was just one date—one fabulously romantic date—but still . . . Maybe it would help with the decision-making process.

My phone rang. After receiving the flowers, I naturally expected it to be Ted. Of course, it wasn't. My gut feeling was way off today.

It was Todd. Guilt flooded through me.

"Hi, there," he said. "Have you spoken with Jason yet?"

"Yes." Jason Daltrey was the name of the FBI agent. "He's planning to meet me at your place at six this evening."

"You sound kind of nervous. Is everything all right?"

"Yeah, it's just been a weird day so far." I told him about Frederic mentioning that David looked familiar and that when I put a face to the name,

Frederic said David had worked for the Santiago Corporation.

"Did you mention that to Jason?" Todd asked.

"No. I e-mailed Riley about it and asked her to look into it. I'm hoping Frederic is wrong." I sighed. "We agreed it would be a strange coincidence for an employee of the Santiago Corporation to be visiting me just after his mother was killed."

"But David got into town before Ms. Ortega was stabbed."

"Right," I said, "but the morning of her death, he got here shortly after I did."

"But so did Sadie and I," Todd reminded. "We were concerned about you. Not that I'm trying to defend David, by any means. Have you heard back from Riley yet?"

"Not yet," I replied. "I'll check my e-mail again before I meet with Agent Daltrey."

After talking with Todd, I called to thank Ted for the flowers. The call went to voice mail, so I left him a message. I didn't mention the masquerade ball. I thought it was best to accept his invitation in some way other than a voice mail message. I did, however, throw away the rose David had left me earlier in the week. It looked wilted and sad beside Ted's bouquet.

Just before closing time, a woman hurried in clutching a tote bag. I stood and put aside the Kuba cloth quilt.

"Hi," I said. "How can I help you?"

She opened the tote bag and took out a cross-stitch piece she'd completed. It was a lovely landscape of a meadow in springtime.

"This is beautiful," I said.

"Thank you. But what can I do about this?" she asked, pointing to a ring left by the embroidery hoop.

"It isn't terribly bad. I have a solution of water and white vinegar that might help. Either have a seat or look around the shop while I see what I can do." I went into my office and took a small ironing board, an iron, and a spray bottle of water and white vinegar solution out of the closet. I plugged in the iron. While it heated up, I called to the customer and asked if she'd like a cup of coffee or tea.

"No, thank you," she called back. "You have some wonderful pattern books."

"Thank you." I licked the middle finger of my left hand and tapped it quickly to the bottom of the iron. It was almost there. I sprayed the backside of the fabric lightly with the water and vinegar solution and then pressed it with the iron. I turned the fabric over. It took one more spray application and pressing before the ring disappeared. I turned off and unplugged the iron before taking the cross-stitched landscape back to the customer.

She was relieved. "I appreciate your help so much. Do I owe you anything?"

"Of course not. I'm just glad I could help."

She bought a couple pattern books before leaving.

I rang up the sale, turned off the lights, and locked the doors. Then Angus and I left. I now needed to rush in order to get him home and get back to the Brew Crew by six o'clock to meet with Agent Daltrey.

As I was driving, my phone rang. It was Riley.

"Hi," she said. "I've been looking into David's employment background. His last job was with the Santiago Corporation."

"When did it end?" I asked.

"A couple weeks ago."

"That's good," I said. "Right?"

"Expound, please."

Riley and her lawyerly phrases. "It means he didn't come here to spy on Francesca Ortega or do anything for the Santiago Corporation, right?"

"Not unless he hoped to get back in the CEO's good graces by doing some freelance work," she said.

"No," I said. "I can't believe that. Or, at least, I can't until I talk with David about it. I have to believe this is all a weird coincidence. David might be a lot of things, but he isn't a murderer."

"I've never met the man, so I'll have to take your word on that one. Just be careful."

* * *

I made it back to the Brew Crew at five fifty-seven p.m. Todd was talking with a man in a navy blue suit. He waved me over, so I guessed the man was Agent Daltrey. From behind, the man looked smaller than I'd thought he would be. I was expecting an Agent Booth (okay, so Mom had got me thinking about David Boreanaz) or at least an Agent Mulder . . . or was it Agent Scully? I never could keep those two straight.

When I reached the bar, Agent Daltrey turned and held out his hand. After I shook the man's hand, I glanced at Todd. They were roughly the same age, but Todd would make two of Agent Daltrey. I always thought FBI agents were large and imposing. This man with his receding hairline, wire-rimmed glasses, and shy smile looked more like a computer genius. Maybe he was. Maybe that's the division of the FBI he worked within.

"It's a pleasure to meet you, Agent Daltrey," I said. "Thank you for coming."

"The pleasure is mine, Marcy. And please call me Jason."

"Can I get you two something to drink?" Todd asked. "It's on the house."

"In that case, I'll have a diet soda," I said, with a grin. "And make it a double."

"Make mine a regular," Jason said.

"Is it okay to talk here?" I asked, looking around the crowded pub.

"You're welcome to use my office," Todd said.

"Why don't we do that?" Jason asked. "Todd, show us the way."

I'd never been in Todd's office, so I was eager to see what it looked like. It was neater than I'd expected it to be. Not that Todd was a slob or anything, but I thought the bar itself would take precedence over the office and administrative duties in his estimation. There was a large walnut desk in the middle of the floor. He had two black desk trays stacked on top of each other. Both trays had some papers in them, making me think they were his in and out boxes. A large cup resembling the cap from a red ballpoint ink pen held a variety of pens and pencils. An electric calculator occupied the right-hand corner of the desk, and a stack of notepads were on the left. A calendar was in the middle of the desk. I noticed the date of the masquerade ball had been circled.

Uh-oh.

Jason took a seat behind the desk, and I sat in the one chair in front of the desk. Jason immediately took one of the notepads off the stack and a pen from the pencil cup.

"I'll check back on you guys in a few minutes," Todd said. He gave me a quick kiss on the cheek before leaving the office and pulling the door closed behind him.

I immediately looked down at my folded hands. I felt so guilty! It wasn't like Todd and I had any sort of agreement. And he hadn't asked me to the masquerade ball. We'd been on a few dates, but it wasn't anything serious.

"What's that about?" Jason asked.

I raised my head. "Excuse me?"

"Why did Todd kissing your cheek make you uncomfortable?"

My eyes darted around the room. "Because you're here? And I don't know you?"

"No, that's not it. Are you seeing someone else?"

I gaped. And then I stammered, "W-we—Todd and I—we aren't in a serious relationship. We date . . . on occasion . . . but neither of us is ready to . . . commit."

Jason nodded. "Or, at least, you're not. But you're afraid Todd might be." He shrugged. "That's between the two of you. I was just curious, that's all."

Wow. FBI people really are incredibly perceptive—or, at least, this one was. It was kind of spooky.

"Let's get to the jewelry." He took some photographs out of the breast pocket of his sport coat. "Concentrate on the stones, not on the actual pieces, and tell me if any of these look like what you saw." He placed the photographs on the desk in front of me.

I leaned in to get a better look at the jewelry. "*Ooh*, I love this necklace." There was a photograph showing a close-up of a triple strand of diamonds and pearls interrupted by larger cabochon blue sapphires. "It's beautiful."

Beside the close-up of the necklace was one of a bracelet that was obviously a companion piece. It, too, had three strands of diamonds, pearls, and blue sapphires. I could imagine myself wearing the necklace and bracelet as part of my masquerade ball ensemble.

"Are there matching earrings?" I asked.

"Marcy, please look at the stones and tell me if they could be the ones you were using to embellish Cassandra Wainwright's wedding gown." He took a small case from his pocket, opened it, and removed a magnifying glass. "Maybe this will help you see the stones independent of their settings." He handed me the magnifying glass.

I peered through the magnifying glass at the stones. The sapphires could be the ones Francesca Ortega had delivered to the shop to be put on the gown. The pearls and diamonds were consistent with the gemstones she had brought as well. But that didn't necessarily mean they came from these pieces. Did it?

"Are they the ones you were working with?" Jason asked.

"I don't know," I said. "They could be. But there were also some larger pearls."

"We haven't looked at everything in the collection yet. But you believe the sapphires you saw could have been the ones composing this necklace and this bracelet. Is that correct?"

I raised my eyes to his. "I can't say for certain, but, yes, it looks like them."

"Very well. Let's move on to the pearls." He gathered the photographs of the triple-strand necklace and bracelet and returned them to his pocket.

He took out a photograph of a pearl necklace. The pearls graduated in size from a sixteen-millimeter center pearl to five-millimeter pearls at the clasp.

I looked at the pearls through the magnifying glass, but I was conflicted. "These might be the pearls I used or they might not. I'm not a jeweler. I thought the stones Ms. Ortega brought in were from a craft or beading supply shop."

"I realize that," Jason said. "All I'm asking you is whether or not the stones in the pieces I've shown you were like the ones you were using or that you saw."

"Okay. Then, yes, they are."

"Now, are you ready to learn where these stones came from?" he asked.

"Maybe." Something in his voice told me I might not be.

Todd opened the door and stuck his head in. "How're you guys doing? Need more sodas?"

Jason shook his head. "Nope, I'm good. Thanks."

"I'm fine, too," I said. "Thank you."

Todd tilted his head. "Are you sure?" He glanced from me to Jason and back again. "You look a little pale, Marce. Are you feeling all right?"

Guilt, guilt, double guilt.

I gave him a tight smile. "I'm fine."

"I was just getting ready to tell her where I think the jewels might've come from," Jason said. "Want to push up the door and stay?"

"Sure." Todd pulled another chair over next to mine. It was a folding chair that had been in the corner. I hadn't noticed it before. He sat down and took my hand.

His hand was warm and strong. My hand felt nice ensconced in his. I squeezed Todd's hand, glad he was here. I didn't know Jason, and he was making me a little uncomfortable with all his suspenseful buildup about where the jewelry had come from. Besides that, Jason knew I was keeping something from Todd. I didn't look at Jason when I squeezed Todd's hand. I kept my eyes focused on the photograph of the pearl necklace.

"So, where do you think the jewels came from?" Todd asked Jason.

"According to our JAG database—that's the FBI's Jewelry and Gem Database—these pieces were among jewelry reported stolen by a Mrs. June Santiago in October of last year."

Now I did look at Jason. "I'm guessing June Santiago is related to the Santiagos who own the Santiago Corporation?"

"She's the matriarch," Jason said. "She's married to Caleb Sr."

"And you think the jewels Francesca Ortega brought me to adorn Cassandra's dress were taken from the necklaces and bracelet you showed me?" I asked.

"Yes, I do."

I shook my head. "But I had dinner with Caleb Santiago Jr. on Saturday evening, and I asked him about the jewels. He never said anything about his mother's jewelry being stolen."

"Maybe he was being evasive," Jason said, picking up the photograph of the pearl necklace and putting it in his pocket with the others. "After all, he doesn't know you. He couldn't be sure what you might be after."

"But he wasn't interested in anything I had to say until I mentioned the jewels," I protested. "That's when he said he'd talk with me after his meeting."

Jason inclined his head. "Still, wealthy people like the Santiagos run into a lot of people who want various things from them. What did he tell you when you asked him about the jewels?"

"Not much. He said he suspected Francesca Ortega might have stolen them with the help of her son, Frederic," I said.

"I need to speak with Frederic," Jason said. "Do you have a number where I can reach him?"

"Wait." I ran my free hand through my hair in

exasperation. "I talked with Frederic earlier today. He was going to go through his mother's apartment and see what he could find."

"Then you believe Frederic is innocent," Todd said.

"I think he's innocent of his mother's murder," I said. "He obviously loved her very much. As for the jewelry, who knows? But I'm in a better position to find out than you are if you just start questioning him, Agent Daltrey. Besides, his mother's funeral is in the morning."

Jason sighed. "I know the timing is off. But with Frederic's mother dead and her funeral dispensed with, he and his fiancée would have no reason to stay here and be convicted of jewel theft after tomorrow. I won't let him get away."

"Can't you just follow him to make sure he sticks around after the funeral?" I asked. "Give me tomorrow to see what information I can find out, and then you can question him."

"Are you kidding me?" Jason spread his hands. "I'm a federal agent. You have no control over what I do."

"I realize that." I dropped Todd's hand and stood. I placed both hands on the desk and leaned toward Jason. "And I'm not trying to control what you do. I'm just asking you to be compassionate and to give me a chance to find out what I can from Frederic before you scare him off."

"She is good at finding things out," Todd told Jason. "This isn't her first investigation."

Jason blew out a breath. It was cinnamony, a fact for which I was grateful since his face was so close to mine. "One day. After that, I'm talking to Frederic myself."

Chapter Fifteen

As soon as I got home, I went through the house to the back door to let Angus in. He was excited and playful. I hung up my coat and then threw his tennis ball down the hall for him time after time until he calmed down a little.

When he was relaxed enough to lie at my feet and chew on a rubber bone, I checked my phone messages. I'd heard back from Ted. He said he'd try to reach me again later but that if he didn't, he'd see me tomorrow.

Mom had called. I knew I should call her back, but I put it off until tomorrow. I dreaded telling her about Francesca Ortega. After all, Mom was in New York, and I didn't want her to catch the first plane out when there was nothing she could do, anyway.

I called David, and he answered on the first ring.

"David Frist," he said.

"You sound very official," I said.

"Sorry." He chuckled. "I didn't recognize your number, and I thought it might be someone calling me about a job. You wouldn't believe how many résumés I've sent out."

"Why didn't you tell me you used to work with Frederic Ortega?" I asked.

"*Um* . . . who? Frederic Ortega?"

"Yes. You remember, don't you? He was in my shop the other morning because his mother was killed on the sidewalk outside the Seven-Year Stitch."

"Oh yeah," David said. "I thought that guy looked familiar. Man, I can't believe I didn't put the face with the name sooner."

"He recognized you, too. He said you worked at the Santiago Corporation together."

"Right." He drew the word out. "Small world, *huh*? So, *um*, did you think about what we spoke about yesterday—relocating to San Fran?"

"I don't think so. I'm happy here, David."

"Maybe I need to expand my job search to include Oregon, then. Or call off the job search altogether and go into business with you."

"I'm not in the market for a business partner," I said. Furthermore, I didn't want to argue with

David tonight. "I need to go. I've got a busy day tomorrow."

"Too busy to have dinner with me?"

"I'm afraid so." I could've been cordial enough to suggest another evening, but I didn't want to have dinner with David. I'd tried to make it clear to him that he and I were through. "Good night."

"Talk with you in a day or so."

"Good night," I repeated, and ended the call.

I still didn't believe David was a murderer. But I was becoming more and more convinced that his being in Tallulah Falls had less to do with me and more to do with the Santiago Corporation.

I wouldn't say Tuesday was a sunny day, but at least it wasn't raining. I was glad of that for Frederic's sake. The funeral was at eleven o'clock. I planned to be at the shop by nine thirty and post a note that I'd be out from eleven until noon. I put on a black wool suit with a white silk blouse and left Angus playing in the backyard. Once again, getting into the Jeep wearing a pencil skirt was not an easy task. I sometimes regretted not buying a snazzy little sports car instead of the Jeep, but Angus would never fit into a sports car.

Even though it wasn't raining, it was cold. The first thing I did when I got to the shop was turn up the heat. I kept a pair of ballet flats stashed in my office, so I exchanged my stilettos for those while I worked. I replenished the yarn bins, and I made note of the colors I was getting low on. I didn't want to overbuy, though, because spring was just around the corner. I'd probably need to invest in some lighter-weight yarns.

The purse Vera wanted me to make for her led me to believe a ribbon embroidery display would be a good idea. I decided to make two ribbon embroidery purses and create a window display using the purse I wasn't giving to Vera. I could add an assortment of ribbon and a couple of books on ribbon embroidery. I also considered offering a class on ribbon embroidery in the spring. I know a lot of people are intimidated by ribbon embroidery at first because they believe it would be hard to do, but it's surprisingly simple.

I went into the office and printed out a sign saying that I'd gone to a funeral but would be back at noon. I didn't want to merely leave my little clock on the door indicating I'd return at twelve p.m. without further explanation when I was going to be away from the shop for such a long period of time.

I was able to finish up the Kuba cloth quilt before I had to leave, and I was happy about that. Now I could get the quilt to the Lincoln City antique festival next week and, hopefully, get some good publicity for the Seven-Year Stitch.

The funeral was being held at the graveside. Although it wasn't raining today, it had done enough yesterday to ensure that the ground was a muddy mess. Having put back on my stilettos, I slid out of the Jeep and instantly sank, oh, about four inches. Fortunately, Ted had been watching for me. He came over, put one arm around my waist, and lifted me out of the mud.

"I think I just plucked the fairest flower in the garden," he whispered, barely suppressing a laugh.

The funeral director had placed green indoor-outdoor carpet around the casket. The carpet allowed them to place three rows of chairs facing the casket and the flowers behind it.

"Can you just help me get over there to that carpet?" I asked. "I can stand behind the chairs until the service is over."

With the arm he had around my waist, Ted picked me up and strode over to the carpeted area. He set me down but kept his arm around me to steady me.

Harriet—in sensible detective shoes—came to stand beside us. She handed me a tissue. "For the mud."

"Thanks." I took the tissue and cleaned the mud off my heels, grateful that Ted was still supporting me with his strong right arm. Then I looked around for something to do with the tissue. Harriet handed me another. I folded the dirty tissue into the clean one and dropped it into my purse.

I followed Harriet's gaze to where Frederic and Cassandra were sitting in the front-row-center chairs. Frederic was staring at his mother's coffin. Cassandra was looking at her watch and then looking around to see what the holdup was. She was obviously eager to get the funeral over with.

Harriet shook her head in disgust. "She doesn't care about him. She only cares about herself."

"He knows that," I whispered. "I don't think he'll marry her."

She turned toward me, her eyes sparkling with interest. "Really? You don't think so?"

"We'll talk later." I was glad the rookie detective was treating me with some emotion other than disdain, but this wasn't the time or the place to discuss Frederic's relationship.

A black limousine pulled up. A chauffeur exited the car and opened the door for Caleb Santiago Sr. Mr. Santiago, walking with a cane, struggled over to sit in a chair near Frederic. He leaned over and said something to Frederic, and Frederic nodded.

I looked up at Ted, who gave a slight shrug.

Several more people arrived. I was looking around at the other grave sites when I felt Ted's arm tighten around my waist. I glanced up to see that his hard gaze was fixed somewhere to my left. I followed his gaze to see David. He was speaking with Mr. Santiago.

When I recovered from my shock, I hissed, "What's he doing here?"

"*Shh,*" Ted said. "They're about to begin."

After a brief, emotional service, the mourners began to disperse. I didn't see David among them.

"Take me over to Frederic," I said to Ted.

"All right."

Even though the carpet was there, the ground was still soft and uneven. Ted helped me keep my balance as we walked. Harriet went with us.

"I'm so sorry," I said to Frederic.

"Thank you." He hugged me and whispered, "We'll talk in a while."

I nodded.

Frederic hugged Harriet, too. Cassandra didn't even shake anyone's hand. She appeared to be irritated by the intrusion.

"Frederic, we should have lunch now, don't you think?" she asked.

"Yeah. Sure." Frederic held Harriet's eyes a moment before squeezing her hand. "I'll talk with you later, Harriet. Thank you for everything."

Mr. Santiago was waiting for his chauffer to come and escort him to the car.

I held out my hand. "Hello, Mr. Santiago. I'm Marcy Singer. We spoke on the phone a few days ago."

"Of course," he said. "Thank you for calling me, Marcy. I appreciate your thoughtfulness. May

I buy you dinner this evening? I'm only in town the one night, and I hate to dine alone."

"I'd love to, Mr. Santiago."

"Please give your address to my chauffeur." He nodded. "He's on his way over here now."

When the chauffeur arrived, I gave him a card with the address of the shop. Mr. Santiago said he'd pick me up at five thirty, and I told him that would be great.

Ted and Harriet walked me to the Jeep.

Ted lifted me into the driver's seat. "What're you up to, Inch-High?"

I ignored his question and spoke to Harriet. "He calls me Inch-High Private Eye. That's not very flattering, is it?"

"I'm with him. What are you up to?"

"Can you come by the shop?" I asked.

"We'll bring lunch," Ted said. "Chicken salad croissant from MacKenzies'?"

"Sounds great. See you in a few."

As soon as I got to the shop, I began calling the students in tonight's class and canceling. I was on my last one when Ted and Harriet came into the shop. I held up an index finger for them to give me a minute to finish my call.

"That's right," I said. "Same time next week. Sorry for any inconvenience."

Ted set the bag from MacKenzies' Mochas on the coffee table. "We didn't get drinks."

"I have sodas in my minifridge," I said as I

pressed the button to end my call. "What would you like?"

"Let me see what you have," he said.

"A diet soda would be great if you've got it," Harriet said.

"Let me see what you have?" I mocked once he and I were alone in the office. "Could you be more obvious?"

He chuckled and pulled me to him for a hug. "The flowers look good."

"They're gorgeous. Thank you."

"So, will you go with me to the masquerade ball?" he asked.

"I'd love to."

"Is there anything you need to tell me that you can't talk about in front of Harriet?" Ted asked.

"Yes. You're cute."

He rolled his eyes. "You know what I mean."

"Do you trust her?"

He nodded.

"Then that's good enough for me," I said. I took two diet sodas from the fridge and let Ted look for himself. There was diet soda, regular soda, and mango juice. He chose a mango juice, and we returned to the sit-and-stitch square.

Harriet was sitting in one of the chairs, so Ted and I sat on the sofa facing the window.

"At the funeral, you said you didn't think Frederic would marry Cassandra," Harriet said. "Why is that?"

"He pretty much said so. When he was here yesterday, he said he loved her but that he didn't think she was right for him. He doesn't think their priorities are the same." I shrugged. "I told him it was better to find that out before the wedding than after."

"I don't think Cassandra truly loves Frederic," she said. "If she did, she'd put his feelings first. She wouldn't be able to even think of having a wedding so soon after his mother died."

"I agree. She's cold," I said.

"Do you think she's cold enough to kill someone?" Harriet asked.

"I don't know." I opened my soda and took a drink. "Ted, why do you think David was at the funeral?"

"I'd have thought he was just following you until I saw him speaking with Santiago," Ted said. "Which brings me to your dinner date this evening. What's up with that?"

"You heard him. He's only in town for the evening. He hates to dine alone." I glanced at him from the corners of my eyes.

"Not buying it," he said. "You're usually not that quick to cancel your classes."

I opened the bag. "Whose sandwich is whose?"

"Marcy." There was a serious tone in his voice.

I quit digging through the bag. "Okay. Todd fixed me up with this FBI agent."

"Calloway fixed you up?" he asked.

"Not that kind of fixed up," I said. "Arranged a meeting. Anyway, the guy is a jewel expert and wants to talk with Frederic. He thinks Frederic had something to do with the stolen jewels Francesca had. The agent believes Francesca stole some jewelry from Mrs. Santiago, and I only have one day to find some answers."

Ted pressed his fingertips into his temples. "Back up, start from the beginning, and go slowly."

"Okay." I relayed to Harriet and Ted how Todd had called and told me he had a friend with the FBI who might be able to discover if the jewels Francesca had given me to put on the dress were stolen. The agent—Jason Daltrey—had called me, asked about the jewels, and had linked them to some jewelry stolen from Mrs. Santiago. I said that Caleb Santiago Jr. never mentioned that any of his mother's jewelry had been stolen. I also told Ted and Harriet how Frederic cued me in to the fact that David Frist had recently worked for the Santiago Corporation.

"I'm with you so far," Ted said. "But how does all this translate into your having one day to find answers?"

"The agent wanted to talk with Frederic last night," I said. "I told him that the funeral was today and asked him to have some compassion. Besides, I kinda told Frederic that Caleb Santiago Jr. might be setting him up—which he might be—

and Frederic was going to look around at his mother's house to see if he could find any evidence of where the jewels came from."

"You're afraid that if the federal agent gets involved, Frederic won't help you anymore," Harriet said.

"You're in over your head, Marcy," Ted said. "Let the investigators do the investigating. Give me Agent Daltrey's number. Harriet and I will take it from here."

"But I think I can get more help from Frederic than the government can because the government sees him as a suspect," I said.

"He is a suspect," Ted said.

"True, but everyone's a suspect." I grinned. "Besides, if Frederic is guilty, he'll be more likely to let something slip to me than to you or an FBI agent."

Ted sighed, snatched up the MacKenzies' bag, and asked, "Whose sandwich is whose?"

Sometimes he knew better than to argue.

Chapter Sixteen

Vera arrived shortly after lunch with the rest of the materials I needed to make her purse. I was eager to get started on it.

I took the black linen and smoothed it out on the coffee table. "This is great. I'll take the gold ribbon and make lots of spiderweb roses, and I'll add accent leaves with the dark green. I'll put some beading on it, too."

"Will it be ready in time to take to the ball?" Vera asked.

"Oh yeah," I said. "I might even have it finished by tomorrow evening's class."

She grinned. "That would be terrific. Everyone will want one . . . Of course, you won't have time to make them, though . . . will you?"

"I'm hoping to make myself one," I said, with a

smile. "But I can assure you, you won't be upstaged at the ball."

"Oh, I—I know. I'll go so you can get to work."

"All right." I was surprised she didn't want to stay and watch, but I was relieved that she didn't. I felt I could do a better job without Vera's scrutiny over every move I made.

As soon as she left, I cut out the pattern for the purse. I then took the front piece and marked my design with a fabric marker. As I'd explained to Vera, most of the design consisted of spiderweb roses, so I made a series of what looked like asterisks across what would ultimately be the front of the purse. I then got some sturdy gold thread and outlined the asterisks. I was preparing to weave the satin ribbon through the threads when Frederic came into the shop.

He had changed from the suit he'd worn to the funeral to faded jeans and a red sweatshirt. He flopped onto the sofa and sighed. "I found gemological certificates at Mom's house. She knew the gems were real."

"So she'd had them appraised," I said.

He nodded.

"Did you find any tools—anything to indicate that she'd taken pieces of existing jewelry for the gems?"

"No." He frowned. "Why do you ask?"

"Maybe they were hers." I shrugged. "Isn't it possible she had some jewelry you didn't know about, and she took it apart to provide this surprise for your wedding? She could've been planning to tell you about it afterward. You know, some grand gesture you hadn't thought she could afford."

"I'd like to think that, Marcy, but I don't. I don't know what to believe."

"You knew your mother better than anyone," I said. "Is it possible she could've taken them?"

"You mean stolen. You're asking if I believe she stole them." He ran his hands through his thick hair. "No. My mother was a good woman. She wasn't a thief." He looked at me. "And your next question, naturally, is then where did the jewels come from? Trust me, I've been over and over this in my mind, and I don't have a clue."

"Could they have been a gift?" I asked.

He shook his head. "She'd have told me about it."

"Maybe not. Like I said, maybe it was a surprise."

"Well, it certainly was that." He blew out a breath. "Here's the thing. My mother winds up with a pouch of jewels and someone kills her to get them back. How did she get entangled in . . . whatever it was?"

"That's what we need to find out. Have you spoken with anyone else about this? Harriet, maybe?"

"No. Not yet. I—I don't want Harriet to think

my mother was a crook. Because she wasn't. She was a good woman, and she raised me to be an honorable man." His eyes welled with tears.

"I know, Frederic. But we need help figuring all this out. Let me give detectives Nash and Sloan a call."

He nodded his consent. It dawned on me that I had things to say that I couldn't say in front of Frederic, so I said I needed to walk Angus and that I'd make the call while I was walking. I hooked Angus up on his leash, told Frederic I'd be back within five minutes, and walked down the street.

Ted answered on the first ring.

"Hi," I said quietly, even though there was little activity on the sidewalk this afternoon. "Frederic is in my shop. He found appraisal certificates. His mother knew the jewels were real."

"Where did she get them?"

"He doesn't know, and I'm calling because my time is up. If we don't do something, Agent Daltrey will haul Frederic in today."

"I'll give Daltrey a call and see if we can work together on this," Ted said. "After all, the murder occurred in our jurisdiction, and I'd think at this point that crime would trump the jewelry theft, especially . . ." He trailed off.

"Especially since other people could be in danger from the killer?" I asked.

"*Um* . . . yeah."

"It's not like we haven't already had this discussion, you know."

"I know," he said. "I just don't like to think about it."

"That makes two of us. Anyway, Frederic is wanting to talk with you and Harriet. Can you come by, or should I send him there?"

"Why don't you send him to us?" Ted said.

"I'll do that."

"Be careful . . . okay?"

"You, too," I said. Relieved that I didn't have to clean up after Angus after all, I returned to the shop.

"Hi," I said to Frederic as I unleashed Angus. "Thanks for holding down the fort."

He nodded toward a customer who had come in and was browsing.

I went over to the customer, a young woman dressed in a business suit. "Welcome to the Seven-Year Stitch. Please let me know if I can help you find anything."

"Thank you. I will."

As she continued to look around, I returned to Frederic. "Ted and Harriet asked that you drop by their place."

"You mean, now?" he asked.

"As soon as you can. They're eager to talk with you."

"Thanks," he said, rising from the sofa.

"Keep me posted?"

"Sure." He left, and I noticed my customer was ready to check out.

Todd dropped in around three. The store was quiet and serene. Angus was in his bed under the counter, and I was working on Vera's purse in the sit-and-stitch square.

"Hi, there," Todd said.

At the sound of Todd's voice, Angus rose and bounded to him. Todd chuckled and petted the dog's head.

I laughed. "You might as well have announced 'playtime' when you came through the door."

"I guess so," Todd said as Angus raced off and got his tennis ball. Todd rolled the tennis ball for Angus before sitting on the sofa. "Has David been at it again?"

"Huh?" I followed his gaze to the flowers on the countertop. "Oh . . . *um* . . . no. I did see him at the funeral this morning, but he didn't even speak. Of course, Ted and Harriet were there, so maybe that's why he didn't say anything."

"He was at the funeral?"

I nodded. "He spoke to Mr. Santiago . . . Senior. Junior wasn't there. And get this—I'm having dinner with Mr. Santiago this evening."

"How did you manage that?" Todd asked.

I shrugged. "He asked me and said he hates to dine alone. I do kind of wonder what this is really about . . . but I guess I'll find out soon enough."

"Did he send the flowers?"

"No." I decided to simply take a deep breath and take the dreaded plunge. "The flowers are from Ted. He sent them with an invitation to the masquerade ball."

"And you accepted?"

I nodded.

He smiled ruefully. "I should've asked sooner."

"I'm sorry," I said.

"No, it's my fault for dragging my feet. I should've asked you weeks ago, not four days before the ball," Todd said. "I'm the one who's sorry. Save me a dance?"

I smiled. "Of course."

"By the way, I got a call from Jason a little while ago. He said Ted called him and wanted to join forces investigating the Ortega murder and Santiago jewel theft."

"Is Jason going to work with them?" I asked.

"I believe so. Why?"

I crossed my fingers. "Hopefully, I'll find out something useful tonight while dining with Mr. Santiago. Did Jason tell you Frederic found appraisals on the gems?"

"Yeah. He thinks that means she stole the jewels."

"I disagree," I said. "How could one little old lady get past Santiago security and steal the matriarch's jewels?"

"She must have had help," Todd said.

"Exactly. But from whom?"

At five o'clock, I raced home with Angus, fed him, and put him in the backyard. I then ran upstairs and changed into a royal blue dress with trumpet sleeves and silver strappy heels. I touched up my makeup, put my wallet and a lipstick into an evening bag, grabbed my black wool trench coat, and made it back to the shop just as Mr. Santiago's chauffer was arriving.

I parked the Jeep and slid out onto the pavement. I used my key fob to lock the door as I hurried toward the limo.

The chauffer got out of the car and went around to open the door for me. "Perfect timing, Ms. Singer."

"Thank you." I got in, and the driver shut the door. I waited until he got behind the wheel and merged into traffic before striking up a conversation. "Have you worked for Mr. Santiago long?"

"Quite a few years," he said.

"Do you enjoy it?"

"Yes."

"Mr. Santiago seems really nice," I continued, despite his noncommittal attitude.

"Yes, he is."

What could I say that would get this man talking? "What about Caleb Jr. and Nicholas? Do you ever drive them, or are you assigned exclusively to Mr. Santiago Sr.?"

"You're a very curious young lady," he said. "I work solely for the senior Santiago."

"I see. What about Francesca Ortega?" I asked. "Did you ever meet her?"

"On occasion."

"What was she like? I mean, I realize Mr. Santiago Sr. thought well of her, but I'm not sure the rest of the corporation shared his view."

"You'd have to ask them, I suppose," he said.

"How did you feel about her?"

"I had no problem with Ms. Ortega."

I realized he was going to report every word of our conversation—such as it was—to his employer, so I tried to come up with something to explain all the questions. "She died right outside my shop, you know. It was terrible."

No comment from the driver.

"Your job must be exciting," I said, hoping to come across as more of a chatterbox than an inquisitor. "Have you ever met anybody famous?"

"No."

"Not that the Santiago Corporation is a talent agency or anything. It's just that I figured rich, upper-crust people rubbed elbows with some famous folks."

"Be that as it may, my elbows are paid to drive the car."

"Right." There was no way I was going to get

any information out of this guy. I wondered if Mr. Santiago would be as difficult as his driver.

When we arrived at the restaurant—an upscale seafood place—the chauffeur pulled up to the door, put the car in park, and came around to help me out of the backseat.

"Enjoy your meal," he said politely.

"Thank you," I said. "It was nice chatting with you on the drive over."

"Likewise." He opened the restaurant door for me before getting back in the limo and driving away.

A hostess greeted me and took my coat. "Are you Ms. Singer?"

"I am."

"Mr. Santiago is right this way." She led me through the dimly lit restaurant to a corner table where Mr. Santiago was waiting with a glass of white wine.

"Thank you for coming, my dear," Mr. Santiago said, raising his glass. "Please bring Marcy a glass of Pinot Grigio."

"Of course," said the hostess. "Right away."

I sat down across from Mr. Santiago. "Thank you for inviting me."

He waved away my remark with a flick of his hand. "You're doing an old man a kindness."

"I imagine it's been a trying day for you."

He nodded. "It has. Poor Frederic. All he has

now is that woman he's about to marry. She seemed very cold to me." He glanced at me. "Sorry if you're her friend."

"Cassandra isn't my friend. As a matter of fact, I only met her, Frederic, and his mother a few days ago. Is Frederic's father dead?"

"I don't know. He and Frannie had divorced before she ever came to work for me, I believe." His mouth turned down at the corners. "Wasn't in the picture very much when Frederic was growing up . . . at least, not that I can recall."

"That's sad. What about Francesca? Was she a good mother?"

"Oh yes," he said. "She put Frederic first in everything. He was the most important part of her life."

The hostess arrived with my wine and said the waitress would be right over to take our order.

"Do you like shrimp?" Mr. Santiago asked me.

"I love it," I said.

He smiled. "The hostess has assured me that the coconut shrimp served on a bed of steamed rice can't be beat."

"Sounds great."

When the waitress came over to our table, Mr. Santiago ordered the shrimp dish for each of us. I understood the old-school order-for-the-lady deal, but at least Mr. Santiago was more considerate about it than his son had been.

After the waitress had scurried away, Mr. Santiago rested his elbows on the table and leaned forward.

"You said you'd only known Frederic and his mother a few days," he said. "How did you meet?"

I explained about Cassandra wanting me to embellish her wedding dress and that she and Frederic were supposed to get married on Valentine's Day.

"They didn't give you much notice, then, did they?" he asked.

"No, they didn't. I get the impression Cassandra is very headstrong and that what she wants she somehow gets." I smiled. "I have to admit to feeling sorry for Frederic when I think about him spending the rest of his life with that woman."

Mr. Santiago chuckled. "Strong-willed women aren't necessarily bad, Ms. Singer. I get the impression you're pretty high-spirited yourself."

"Maybe just a little. What about Francesca? Was she strong-willed?"

"I would say no," he said, inclining his head slightly. "Frannie wasn't the type to make waves."

"Which makes it even more curious that her mugger killed her," I said. "Wouldn't she have given him her purse without a fight?"

"The Frannie I knew would have. The only thing she'd have ever fought for would have been her son."

"Was she a good administrative assistant?" I asked.

"She was," he said, nodding. "She was thorough and accurate."

"I don't think your son was as impressed. He said she didn't keep up with the times."

He spread his hands. "Frannie had been trained on a typewriter. Word processing software was difficult for her to learn. She managed all right, but not well enough to suit Caleb."

"Frederic said Caleb let Francesca go because he caught her snooping in his desk."

He smiled. "Caleb was right—you don't mince words. I like that."

So the two of them had discussed my meeting with Caleb Jr.

"Caleb values his privacy," Mr. Santiago continued. "I don't know that I'd call whatever Frannie was doing snooping, but Caleb saw it as such."

"But you liked Francesca," I said. "Why did you agree to let her go? Couldn't you have simply transferred her to another department?"

He shook his head. "It was Caleb's call. I couldn't undermine his business decisions, could I? I'd turned the company over to him . . . unconditionally."

"Of course." I took a sip of my wine. "What about the jewels?"

"What about them?"

"The police think they're stolen," I said. "As a

matter of fact, they think the gems might have been taken from jewelry that your wife reported missing."

He arched an eyebrow but said nothing.

"Do you think Francesca Ortega stole some of your wife's jewelry?" I asked.

"I couldn't say. My wife and I haven't lived together in over five years," he said.

"I'm sorry. I didn't realize that."

The waitress arrived with our food, asked if we needed anything, and refilled our wineglasses before leaving.

"This looks delicious," I said.

"It does indeed." He placed his napkin in his lap. "Tell me something, Marcy. Why are you so interested in the jewels Frannie had?"

"I'm afraid that whoever killed her may think I still have some of the gems in my shop." I saw an opportunity to find out what Mr. Santiago might reveal to me about David and his role—or former role—with the Santiago Corporation. "In fact, on the night I met with your son, I was followed to the lodge. It scared the daylights out of me, but it turned out to be only a former boyfriend—David Frist."

Mr. Santiago looked up at that but said nothing.

"I believe David once worked for your company," I said.

"Ah yes." Mr. Santiago nodded as he dug his fork into his rice. "I thought that name sounded vaguely familiar."

"Did you know David well?"

Mr. Santiago put a forkful of rice into his mouth and held up a finger for me to give him a second. It reminded me of the candy bar commercial where people put the food into their mouths because they need a minute to think. Mr. Santiago might want to deny knowing David, but he'd have to realize I saw them together at the funeral earlier today.

He swallowed and took a sip of his wine. "I'd met Mr. Frist on a couple of occasions, but I don't really know him personally." He smiled. "However, I can't say that I blame him for pursuing you. I'd be tempted to do so myself if I were a couple decades younger."

I laughed. "How very flattering." It was obvious I wasn't going to get any more information out of Mr. Santiago.

Chapter Seventeen

You know that old saying, speak of the devil and he appears? Well, guess who was waiting for me when I got home? David.

I pulled into the driveway and saw a black sedan on the street in front of my house. I recognized it as the rental car David had used to follow me to the lodge. I slid out of the Jeep and walked to the driver's side of David's car. Over Angus' barking in the backyard, I asked David what he was doing.

"Waiting for you," he said simply.

"How long have you been here?" I asked.

"A little longer than he has." He nodded toward a patrol car parked down the street facing in our direction.

I turned and walked toward the policeman. He got out of his car, and I recognized him as the young officer who was guarding the crime scene outside my shop the day Francesca Ortega was stabbed.

"Good evening, Ms. Singer," he said. "Is everything all right?"

"I think so, Officer Moore. Thank you for being here."

"You're welcome. Mr. Frist isn't parked in your driveway, so he isn't technically trespassing since he isn't on your land," Officer Moore explained. "However, now that you're here, and especially because he's already been cited for stalking you, I can write him up for trespassing against you personally or for stalking if he doesn't leave."

"Thank you," I said. "But I think everything will be okay and that he'll go on his way after talking with me."

Officer Moore nodded and went back to his car.

I returned to the sedan. David had gotten out of the car and was leaning against it with his arms folded across his chest.

"Did you tell him to get out of here?" he demanded.

"No," I said. "But I did assure him that you'd leave after talking with me. So, what's up?"

"Where've you been?" he asked.

"Dinner." I knew it wasn't any of his business, but this might be a good way to get him to talk about Mr. Santiago and his company. "Actually, I had dinner with a friend of yours . . . Caleb Santiago Sr."

"Friend of mine?" David asked. "Says who?"

"I saw you talking with him at Francesca Ortega's funeral today."

"Oh yeah . . . yeah." He nodded rapidly. "I wouldn't say we're friends, though. I was just paying my respects."

"Since you used to work for him," I said.

"For his son, actually."

"Did you know Francesca?" I asked. "Did the two of you ever work together?"

"No. I worked with Caleb—Junior, that is—but I didn't work directly with Francesca. She was only a secretary," David said.

"Only."

"Hey, I didn't mean it that way." He shrugged. "I just meant she was his secretary, not mine, and I didn't work with her. I knew who she was, but I didn't pay much attention to her."

"Did Caleb talk about why he fired her?" I asked.

"He said she was a snoop and that she wasn't good at her job."

"What did she find while she was snooping?"

"You'd have to ask her or Caleb Jr. But she can't tell you, and I don't think he would because it isn't any of your—or anyone else's—concern." He looked around impatiently. "Are we going inside, or what? It's cold out here."

"No," I said. "We're not going inside. I'll talk with you out here."

"What? Are you afraid I'll murder you or something?"

"I don't know what you might do, David. You haven't been behaving reasonably—or, at least, like the man I thought I knew—the entire time you've been here."

He blew out a disgusted breath. "Oh, get real. You really enjoy playing the damsel in distress, don't you? Having everybody rush to protect you. Poor little Marcy. We have to save her!"

"I won't allow you to manipulate me," I said, walking toward the front door. "Good night."

I knew he'd gotten back in his car because I heard the door slam. Then I heard him speed off down the road. Before placing my key in the lock, I turned and waved to Officer Moore. He blinked his lights for me, but he didn't leave yet. I was kind of glad.

I'd barely had time to get settled in at work the next morning before Ted called. I answered with my typical "Thank you for calling the Seven-Year Stitch."

He interrupted with "Andrew told me David Frist was waiting for you when you got home last night."

"He was," I said, "but it was no big deal. In

fact, I was glad to have the opportunity to ask him a couple questions under Officer Moore's watchful eye."

"Good. Andrew said you wouldn't allow Frist into the house. He didn't come back later, did he?"

"No, Ted, everything was fine. I did ask him about working for the Santiago Corporation and whether or not he knew Francesca Ortega."

"What did he say?"

"He said he hadn't worked directly with Francesca and hadn't paid much attention to her. Since she wasn't some young hottie, I believe that," I said. "He confirmed—almost verbatim—the reasons Caleb Santiago gave for firing her."

I went on to tell Ted about my dinner with Caleb Sr. "Really, the only thing of interest that he disclosed to me was that he hadn't lived with his wife in over five years. That could possibly absolve him of the suspicion of stealing Mrs. Santiago's jewels himself."

"I'll check into it to see what I can determine about their living arrangements," Ted said. "He could still theoretically have taken the jewels, though, out of spite or to provide some sort of severance pay to Ms. Ortega or—"

"Or as a bribe," I said.

"Or that," he agreed. "Maybe these jewels had been kept in a joint safe-deposit box or something. I'll talk with Agent Daltrey and see what he knows."

"How did your meeting with Frederic go yesterday?" I asked.

"He claimed he knew nothing about the jewels. Like you, he conceded the gems that his mother had in her possession could have been the ones from Mrs. Santiago's jewelry."

"Did Agent Daltrey seem to believe him?"

"Hard to say," Ted said. "I think he's telling the truth. I mean, he could know more than he's letting on, but I don't think he aided in stealing the jewels, and I'm almost convinced he had nothing to do with his mother's death."

"Almost?"

"Hey, everyone's—"

"A suspect," I finished with a laugh.

As we completed our call, Sadie came into the shop. She zeroed in on the flowers immediately and went over to sniff them.

"Gorgeous!" she cried. "Did Todd finally get off his butt and invite you to the ball?"

"No," I said. "Ted did."

"Oh."

"Todd already knows. He came by yesterday and saw the flowers." I shrugged. "He said he should've asked sooner, but he wanted me to save him a dance. I guess everything is cool."

"Good." She sat on the sofa. "So, what are you wearing?"

I told her about my trip to Lincoln City with Vera and that I had chosen a white beaded gown over the one Vera had in mind for me. "Vera says my dress looks too much like a wedding gown, but I don't care. I love it. And the mask is awesome!"

Sadie smiled. "That's terrific. I can hardly wait to see it."

I took Vera's purse materials out of my tote bag and continued carefully crafting spiderweb roses. "This will ultimately be the purse Vera will be using to accessorize her dress. It's gold with a black lace inset."

"Sounds pretty," she said. "Sounds like Vera."

"Yeah. I told her I'd try to have the purse done for her this evening."

"It looks like it's going well."

"It is. So, barring any interruptions . . ."

She frowned. "Is that a hint?"

"Never," I said. "I don't consider you an interruption. I'm just guessing David might be by today after the scene outside my house last night."

"What has he done now?" she asked, with a growl creeping into her voice.

I explained how he was waiting on me when I got home from having dinner with Mr. Santiago. "He's being really creepy, Sadie. He wasn't like that when I dated him before—was he?"

"I don't think so," she said, "but then, I didn't know him all that well. Maybe you didn't, either. Be careful where he's concerned."

"I will."

After Sadie left, I pondered the strangeness of the entire situation with Francesca Ortega as I worked. The facts, as I knew them, were: Francesca had worked for the Santiago Corporation for more than twenty years. She'd originally worked with Caleb Sr., who had given her a glowing report, but had been fired by Caleb Jr., who accused her of snooping. Had Francesca found something that Caleb—Junior or Senior—would kill to keep her from revealing? Riley had said the business appeared to be involved in some shadier practices since Junior took the helm.

And what did any of that have to do with the gems that might or might not have come from June Santiago's jewelry box? Had one of the Santiago CEOs given the jewels to Francesca? Had he done so to buy her silence or to enhance her severance package without anyone seeing a large monetary disbursement on the books? Was it to collect the insurance money? Or had someone given her the jewels with the intention of making her look like a thief and prosecuting her once Mrs. Santiago reported the jewelry stolen? If that person wanted the insurance money and wanted to frame Francesca, that would be an excellent way to achieve his or her goals.

Or had Francesca, in fact, stolen the jewels? She couldn't have been looking forward to living with Cassandra Wainwright. I could see Cassandra making her mother-in-law miserable. Of course, I didn't know Francesca. Maybe she'd have made Cassandra miserable. But even if Francesca had stolen the gems from Mrs. Santiago, she'd have had to have had help from someone . . . someone on the inside.

The bells over the shop jingled, and I was glad to put Vera's purse and my ruminations aside to provide assistance. The woman was looking for some cross-stitch pattern books, and I cheerfully fixed her up with two excellent options for the holiday theme she was looking for.

She hadn't been gone long, and I'd barely had time to make any substantial progress on Vera's purse before Frederic came in. He was carrying a drink tray, which he nearly dropped when Angus loped over to greet him. I put the purse aside and scrambled to help Frederic.

"Angus, down," I said. The dog still kept bouncing in front of Frederic. I took the drink tray from him and set it on the counter. "Angus, down." I gave the command in a firmer tone this time, and Angus finally did as he was told. "Sorry about that," I said to Frederic.

"It's all right. At least he was glad to see me. That's more than I can say for Cass yesterday when I got home from the meeting at the police station."

"She was probably worried about you," I said.

Frederic scoffed. "Hardly. She flew into telling me about all the plans she needed to finalize for the wedding and that I wasn't there when she needed me . . . that I needed to pull my share of the weight." He shrugged. "I told her the wedding was off."

"Oh my gosh! What did she say?"

"I'm not sure. As she began yelling, she threw a vase at me. Fortunately, it missed my head and broke against the wall behind me. Then I simply left. She obviously had nothing rational to say, and I wasn't in the mood to either listen or to try to placate her."

Angus lost interest in our conversation and went to lie by the window in the sun.

"How did the interview at the station go?" I asked.

"As well as could be expected, I guess." He stepped to the counter and handed me one of the drinks. "It's from MacKenzies' Mochas. The guy there said this was your usual."

"Low-fat vanilla latte with a hint of cinnamon," I said.

He nodded. "That's it. Mine's a cappuccino." He took his drink, and we sat in the sit-and-stitch square. "The FBI guy thinks I'm guilty."

"Of what?" I asked, taking the lid off my latte and inhaling its sweet aroma.

"Of everything," he said. "He made me out to be like some supervillain. He believes I stole the jewels, that I . . ." He shook his head.

I realized he couldn't bring himself to say the

words *killed my mother*. I filled the awkward pause. "But Ted and Harriet were on your side, weren't they?"

"To the extent they could be, I guess. But that guy threw so many questions at me. Where was I the night of October twenty-fourth? Who knows?"

I frowned. "He actually asked you where you were on October twenty-fourth? Was that relevant?"

"The date wasn't actually October twenty-fourth," Frederic said. "I'm being a bit facetious . . . but not much. What I'm getting at is that the guy threw so many questions at me I didn't know whether I was coming or going. By the way, where were you on October twenty-fourth?"

"I don't know," I said. "Was that a weekday or a weekend?"

"I have no idea . . . which is precisely my point."

"What sort of questions did he ask regarding the jewels?"

"He asked if I'd ever met June Santiago," he said. "I told him I had met her once at an office party. He then wondered if I'd admired the jewelry she was wearing that evening. I mean, how ridiculous is that? I don't pay attention to jewelry!"

"I wouldn't think many men would unless the piece was particularly ostentatious or the man was in a business that dealt with jewelry," I said.

"I don't pay attention to details, period," Frederic said. "For example, if I left here right now and someone on the street asked me what you were wearing today, I'd say jeans and a sweater. I don't even know what color to call that sweater, and I have no idea whether or not you're wearing jewelry. Are you?"

I nodded. "Pearl stud earrings. And the sweater is chartreuse, which means it's a mixture of green and yellow."

"I'd have said green. But, anyway, you see where I'm going with this." He took a drink of his cappuccino. "I'm worried, Marcy. I think he's going to charge me with . . . something."

"But if you didn't do anything, then how can he?"

"I don't know." He sighed. "Will you help me?"

"If I can."

He leaned toward me. "I want you to come to Mom's apartment with me. Help me find anything I might've missed."

"Okay." I stretched the word out. This was a huge opportunity to find out more about what Francesca did and didn't know about the jewels or what other reason someone might have had for wanting her dead. On the other hand, I didn't know Frederic well enough to trust him completely. "What if we take Harriet or Ted with us? That way, someone—other than two non-law-enforcement people—will be there to help collaborate what we discover."

Frederic didn't get a chance to respond, because Cassandra stormed into the shop.

"There you are!" she yelled.

Angus jumped up and began barking.

"Cassandra, please calm down," I said. "At least until I can get Angus restrained."

She fumed, but she didn't say anything as I got Angus' leash and led him to the bathroom. I shut him inside, but he scratched at the door and continued to bark and growl.

"How can you stand that beast?" she spat when I returned to the shop.

I felt like telling her that she was the beast, but I didn't want to make matters worse.

She glared at Frederic. "Is she the reason you're calling off our wedding?"

"No," he answered calmly. "You are. You threw a vase at my head hours after I buried my mother, Cass."

"You were late! I'm having to do everything by myself! Do you know how hard that is?" She flailed her arms.

"My mother is dead! Do you know how hard that is?" Frederic cried.

"Of course, but you're using that as an excuse to get close to her!" She pointed to me. "And that . . . that . . . Harry person."

"Her name is Harriet," he said, "and she's trying to help me."

"What about me? Who's trying to help me?" Cassandra demanded.

Over the ruckus of Cassandra and Frederic yelling at each other and Angus barking, I didn't even hear the bells over the door jingle as Ted and Harriet came in.

"What's going on here?" Ted asked. "We heard you guys all the way down the street."

Cassandra and Frederic continued their vociferous debate.

"I said, what's going on here?" Ted yelled.

The formerly engaged couple began talking at once. Again, I missed hearing the bells as a customer slipped in. She was an older lady, and she stood watching the scene before her in slack-jawed silence.

"Enough!" Ted shouted.

"Great job!" I clapped my hands. Looking at the customer, I explained, "Theater practice."

She wrinkled her forehead. "But Tallulah Falls doesn't have a theater troupe."

"Not yet, but we're hoping," I said, with a smile. "What can I help you find?"

"I just need a few skeins of yarn to finish up an afghan," she said.

"Right this way." As I passed Ted, I mumbled, "Please restore order."

I escorted the customer to the yarn displays and was glad everything was comparatively quieter while she shopped. Angus was still barking but not as much as he had been. And Frederic and Cassandra were continuing their argument in hissed whispers. The customer bought skeins of navy and red yarn, gave the sit-and-stitch square one last leery look, and then left. I sighed. She'd probably never be back—and I couldn't blame her.

I put my hands on my hips and faced the group. "I'm letting Angus out of the bathroom. His barking is giving me a headache, and I can't stand it any longer. It would be a really good idea to stop bickering now, because he doesn't like it."

As I walked toward the bathroom, I heard Cassandra say, "If she's letting that thing out, I'm leaving. Frederic, we'll resume our discussion later."

I didn't hear Frederic's response and wasn't even sure he gave one.

Chapter Eighteen

Vera arrived early for class. In fact, she got there before I did. I'd taken Angus home for dinner, and when I returned, Vera was waiting for me in her car. The streetlights were just flickering on, and I was glad she was being cautious.

"Did you get it finished?" she asked as she got out of her car and walked toward me.

"Get what finished?" I teased.

"My purse!" She playfully tapped me with the gloves she'd just removed. "Oh, you!"

I laughed and unlocked the door. "Yep. I think you'll be pleased with it. At least, I am."

Once inside, Vera and I took off our coats. I put them on the coatrack in my office and brought the purse out.

"I just finished it this afternoon," I said.

Vera squealed with delight and hurried over to

take the purse. It had four rows of large ribbon embroidery roses. At random intervals between the roses, green ribbon leaves were evident. I'd also put tiny gold and clear beads on the roses to give the purse more detail and a smidgeon of *oomph*. Vera loved *oomph*.

"It's gorgeous! Thank you so much!" She enveloped me in a one-armed hug and then pulled back to look at the purse again. "Ooh, I don't want anyone else to see it before the ball. Put it back in your office."

"All right. I'll put it in a Seven-Year Stitch bag and set it on the desk. You can grab it when you get your coat." I took the purse from Vera and placed it in a large bag. "Don't forget it," I said when I returned from the office.

"Oh, I won't."

"How did you do on your project this week?" I asked.

"Not as well as you did on yours—I'm talking about the purse, of course." She giggled. "Seriously, Marcy, you did a gorgeous job. Thank you."

"My pleasure. You gave me an idea for a new window display and a new class with the rediscovery of ribbon embroidery. I hadn't done any in a long time."

We didn't have a chance to discuss it further, because the rest of the class began filtering into the shop. Everyone had made significant progress on their needlepoint crafts this week, and we engaged in some lively discussions. But when the rain started coming down amid rumors that it was supposed to get worse as the evening wore on, my class members began to get antsy about getting home and cuddling under a warm blanket. Not that I blamed them. I'd have been happy to do the same thing, but I'd promised Frederic that I'd meet him and Harriet at Francesca's apartment as soon as class was over. On that note, I was glad that the class had ended about half an hour earlier than usual.

As soon as I'd locked up the store, I got into the Jeep and called Frederic. The call went to voice mail, so I told him I was on my way to the apartment. I then plugged his mother's address into my GPS and headed in that direction.

Francesca had lived in a nice neighborhood between Tallulah Falls and Depoe Bay. I wondered if Frederic and Cassandra had planned to move in with her after the wedding, or if Francesca was going to have to give up her apartment. I figured it was Francesca who would have had to make sacrifices either way.

I pulled into the well-lit complex. The buildings had gray vinyl siding, and it appeared each apartment had its own private deck. Although there was a space available right in front of Francesca's door, I left that one for Frederic and Harriet and took a spot two spaces down.

I burrowed my chin into the front of my coat as

I ducked my head, raised my umbrella, and sprinted to the door. I stepped into the entrance hall. A young woman had a baby on her hip and was struggling to juggle a bag of groceries while unlocking her door.

"Need some help?" I asked.

She smiled. "I think I've almost got it. But thanks."

The baby grinned at me, and I waved to her. She raised her little hand in return. Her mother got the door open, and they went inside.

I moved down the hall toward Francesca's apartment. I didn't want the woman with the baby to think I was some kind of nutcase who stood around in apartment hallways. I propped my umbrella against the wall and rubbed my hands together. I felt goofy for forgetting my gloves. I blew into my cupped hands and then rubbed them together again. It was then that I noticed Francesca's door was ajar. Could it be that Frederic and Harriet were already here?

I opened the door and stepped inside the apartment. "Frederic, Harriet, it's me! Where are you?"

The kitchen was to my immediate left. I looked into the room but didn't see Frederic or Harriet, so I went on through to the dining room. The carpet was beige and so plush I sank into it when I stepped out of the kitchen. There was a mahogany table for four with a matching buffet. Over the buffet was an oil portrait of Frederic and Francesca. It was a lovely painting.

I wandered on into the living room. "Guys, where are you?" I was feeling uncomfortable looking around Francesca's apartment by myself. If Harriet and Frederic were here, then why weren't they answering me? I decided to check the rooms at the other end of the hallway. If they weren't there, I'd go back outside the apartment and wait for them.

I went down the hall. The door to my right was open just a bit, much like the door to the apartment had been. I eased into the room. It was a wreck. This bedroom had been converted to a home office. Papers were strewn everywhere, the desk chair had been upended, and the drawers of the file cabinet were open and in complete disarray. It struck me that this was why the door to the apartment had been ajar. Someone had been ransacking Francesca's office. And that someone might still be here.

I started to back out of the room, but I caught a glimpse of something on the floor near the love seat. It looked like . . . a hand . . . a woman's thin, pale hand.

"Harriet?" My voice caught in my throat. I looked behind me to make sure no one was sneaking up behind me, and then I moved closer to the hand. What I saw made me light-headed, and I had to grasp the arm of the love seat to steady myself.

Cassandra Wainright was splayed on the floor, her lifeless eyes turned upward, her mouth slightly agape. She had a stab wound to the sternum, making me think she had been killed by the same person—possibly a professional—who'd killed Francesca. Thoughts began tumbling through my head faster than I could make sense of them. I needed to call 9-1-1. I wondered if I should check to see if Cassandra had a pulse, but would that be contaminating evidence? I should call Frederic and tell him not to come. I swayed and clutched the small sofa for support.

"Marcy!"

I turned to see Harriet standing in the doorway. "What have you done?"

I shook my head. "It wasn't me. The door was open when I got here."

Harriet elbowed past me and knelt beside Cassandra. She placed two fingers on Cassandra's neck; then she moved her hand to Cassandra's wrist. She looked up at me. "She's dead."

"Where's Frederic?" I asked.

"He's right behind me. He should be here—"

"What's going on?"

It was Frederic. I looked at him and then turned back to Harriet.

She stood and walked over to him. "It's Cassandra. She's dead."

"She's what?" He scrambled over to Cassandra's body. "Cass! Cass, wake up." He dropped to his knees beside her.

"Please don't touch her." Harriet took him by the shoulders. "Come on. I need to call this in, and we need to preserve the crime scene."

"But she might still be alive," he said. "Maybe she's just unconscious!"

He tried to turn back to Cassandra, but Harriet kept a firm hold on him. She shook her head. "Let's go into the living room," she said softly.

Harriet, Frederic, and I were in the living room when the county deputies arrived. Harriet flashed her ID and led the officers to the body. There were four deputies—three went with Harriet, and the other one stayed with Frederic and me. Poor Frederic was shaking really hard. I wasn't doing much better, but this guy had lost both his mother and his fiancée within the course of a few days. I didn't know how he was holding it together as well as he was.

The officer who'd stayed behind took out a notebook and pen. He began by asking our full names and why we were in the apartment.

"I'm Frederic Ortega. This is my mom's apartment."

"And where is she?" the officer asked.

I stepped closer to Frederic and placed my hand on his shoulder. "Deceased." I spoke as quietly as I could and still be heard. "The funeral was yesterday."

"And you are?" he prompted.

"I'm Marcy Singer."

He quickly scribbled that in his notebook. "What're you doing here, Ms. Singer?"

I was rather at a loss on what to say to that. My reason for being in the apartment this evening was complicated, and I didn't want to give the deputy a convoluted answer.

This time Frederic answered for me. "I asked Marcy and Harriet—Officer Sloan—to meet me here . . . to help me go through some of Mom's things."

I nodded.

One of the deputies who'd gone into the office with Harriet stepped into the living room and motioned to me. "A word please, Ms. Singer?"

"Of course," I said, walking toward him.

He led me into the hallway. "I understand that you discovered the body."

"That's right."

"Would you please describe the events leading up to that?" he asked.

I told him how I'd arrived, spoken to the young mom, and then came on to Francesca's apartment, where I'd noticed the door was slightly open. I explained how I'd called to Frederic and Harriet and had looked around the house before finding Cassandra.

"Wasn't it apparent that your friends weren't here when they didn't respond to you?" the officer asked. "Why did you continue into the house?"

"I don't know," I said. "Since the door was open, I thought Frederic was here." I folded my arms. "In hindsight, I realize I was reckless in rushing in here without knowing what was going on."

"Why's that?" he asked.

"Because Frederic's mom was stabbed to death on the street outside my shop. And from the look of things, I believe Cassandra was killed by the same person."

"On what do you base your opinion?"

"The two victims knew each other, and they were both stabbed," I said. "Doesn't it stand to reason that their being killed within days of each other is more than a coincidence?"

He ignored my question and asked one of his own. "Prior to your arrival here, where were you?"

"At my shop teaching a needlepoint class. Seven women can attest to my whereabouts."

He nodded. "You may return to the living room. But don't leave."

I went back to the living room and sat on the sofa. Since Frederic passed me in the hallway, I guessed he'd been summoned by Joe Friday. Wasn't Friday the one on that old police drama with the monotone voice who always wanted "the facts"?

The deputy who'd been given witness-sitting duty was making me nervous. He had gorgeous baby blues, but at the moment, I felt like they were boring into my soul.

I nodded toward the photo album on the coffee table. "May I look at this? You know, to pass the time?"

"Yeah," he conceded, "I guess that's all right. You'll be fingerprinted before you leave, anyway, in order to compare your prints to others found in the apartment."

"Good." Not that it was all that good, really, but I was thankful to have something to look at and to hold to help keep my hands from shaking.

I lifted the heavy book off the table and set it on my lap. I opened it and saw that the first photograph was of a baby boy—Frederic. Even though he was very young, I could see the resemblance. I grinned and glanced up at the deputy. He was smiling slightly, too.

"You have children?" I asked.

"One," he said. "A two-year-old son. He's a handful."

I chuckled and turned the page. There were more photos of Frederic. Some were with Francesca and a man who must be—or must have been; I wasn't sure if he was still living—Frederic's father. He looked nice.

As I was flipping through the album, some sort of document fell out onto my lap. I retrieved it and saw that it was a stock certificate from the Santiago Corporation. Had Francesca owned stock in the company, or had she brought this certificate home for some other reason? I thought about the ransacked office and wondered what Cassandra—or her killer—had been looking for in that room.

The coroner arrived. Following closely behind him was Ted.

He hurried into the living room and showed his badge to the deputy. "Detective Ted Nash, Tallulah Falls Police Department." His eyes searched mine before he continued. "My partner and I are investigating the murder of Francesca Ortega. Since we believe Ms. Wainright's death may be connected to that homicide, we'd like to be kept up to speed on this investigation."

"Of course, Detective Nash."

"May I have a word with Ms. Singer out in the hallway?" Ted asked.

"Sure."

I closed the photo album and returned the book to the coffee table before following Ted into the hallway. He opened the door, and we stepped out into the corridor.

He closed the door and took both my hands in his. "Are you okay?"

I smiled slightly. "I'm fine. I got here ahead of Harriet and Frederic, saw that the door was open, and came on in. I found Cassandra." My smile faded. "Which makes me the county cops' prime suspect."

"Harriet said the stab wound matched the one found on Francesca."

I nodded. "One stab to the sternum."

He squeezed my hands. "You'll be all right. I'd better get back in here and confer with Harriet. We'll talk later."

We went back into the apartment, and I returned to the living room. By that time, Frederic was back. He was sitting in the middle of the couch wringing his hands. I sat down beside him.

"This is my fault," he said. "If we hadn't argued, she wouldn't have been here alone."

"You can't possibly know that," I said. "Is this where you and Cassandra were living?"

"No. Our apartment is . . . was—it was Cass's place—it's closer to Tallulah Falls."

"Then what was she doing here?" I noticed that the deputy was listening intently while trying to appear as if he weren't paying attention to us.

"I don't know." Frederic ran his hands through his hair. "Maybe she'd intended to do the same thing we had . . . find something that would lead us to Mom's killer."

Ted returned to the living room. "The coroner has given us a rough estimate of three to six hours on the time of death."

The deputy looked at me and Frederic. "Then

after the two of you are fingerprinted, you're free to go."

"Thank you." I followed the officer to the kitchen, where he placed an ink pad and fingerprint papers on the counter.

"If you'll permit me to roll your fingers, it'll give us a better print," he said.

"Sure."

I allowed the deputy to place each one of my fingers on the ink pad and then roll them into blocks provided on the form.

"That should do it," he said. "You can wash your hands there at the sink."

I washed my hands and returned to the living room, where Frederic still sat on the sofa.

"I'm going to wait here," he said, "for a while, anyway."

"Call me if you need me," I said. I gave Ted a look that I hoped would convey "call me as soon as you leave here." And then I left. I was eager to get home and away from yet another crime scene.

Chapter Nineteen

When I got home, there was a patrol car parked near my house. The driver flashed his lights at me as I got out of the Jeep. I was glad Ted still had his officers looking out for me, especially since I now knew without a doubt that Francesca's killer was still hanging around racking up victims. I unlocked the door, went inside, and immediately refastened the locks. I then brought Angus in from the backyard. I sank onto the floor beside him, and he placed his head in my lap.

Poor Cassandra . . . I wondered why she'd been in the apartment. Had she been looking for something? Or had she come in and surprised the killer? Maybe he'd been looking for more jewels . . . or something else.

I shuddered and snuggled closer to Angus.

Tears pricked my eyes as I thought of Cassandra—snotty, yes, but lively—flouncing into the shop making demands about her dress and grouching about Angus. I contemplated Frederic sitting on the sofa at the shop so devastated about his mother now having to face another loss. I wondered about the killer who was still out there willing to destroy anyone who got in his way. I even considered that young mother and her baby. They'd had no idea how close they'd been to a murderer.

I felt guilty that I'd once imagined Cassandra might've had wanted Francesca dead. How could I have been so quick to rush to judgment? What was it the crime writer had said on that television show I'd seen a while back? People kill for three reasons: for love, for money, or to cover up a crime. So, which was this?

My doorbell rang. I stiffened, and Angus jumped up to run barking into the foyer. I went to the door and peeped out. It was Ted. I let him in, and we went into the living room. Sensing our somber mood, Angus instantly became subdued and simply lay on the floor near the sofa where Ted and I sat.

"How's Frederic?" I asked.

"As well as can be expected, I suppose." Ted clasped his hands behind his head. "He was still at the apartment when I left, although the county deputies were trying to get him to leave."

"You don't . . . you don't think . . ." The

thought seemed so far-fetched—so awful—I could barely bring myself to vocalize it. "He didn't do it. Did he?"

Ted sighed. "He doesn't have the background that would lead me to think he could kill a person with a single, precise knife thrust. And to have killed Cassandra would mean he also murdered Francesca." He unclasped his hands and ran them down his face. "While I can imagine a scenario wherein Frederic stabbed his lover during an argument, I can't see him hurting his mother."

"Neither can I. In fact, I have trouble imagining him being capable of flying into a rage and killing Cassandra," I said. "The poor man must've had the patience of Job to put up with her as long as he did." My hand flew to my mouth. "I'm sorry. I didn't mean that."

"It's okay. You're just trying to reason this out. We all are."

"So, did the county coroner compare the wounds or do whatever needed to be done to confirm that Cassandra and Francesca were murdered by the same person?"

"He and our coroner were able to agree that both women suffered the exact same type of fatal injury," Ted said. "Of course, neither can point us toward a suspect. That's my job."

"And other than your standard 'everyone's a suspect' spiel, do you have anyone in mind?"

He slowly shook his head. "Basic criminology

points to Frederic. He knew both victims intimately, he was the only one who stood to gain anything from his mother's death, and he'd just broken off his engagement to Cassandra. Still, he doesn't have experience in medicine or the military, as far as I know. And besides that, my gut is telling me he didn't kill them."

"While I agree with your gut, I sure wish it would give you a clue," I said. "I want this guy off the streets."

"No worse than I do, Marce."

"Wanna bet?"

I left Angus at home the next morning, and before going in to work, I stopped by Riley's house. Her husband, Keith, was on his way out the door when I arrived.

"How is she?" I asked.

"Stubborn," he said with a grin. "Go on in. She's in the bedroom at the top of the stairs and to your right."

"Thanks." I went inside. The house was immaculate. Either Keith, Riley's mom, or a cleaning crew was doing a fantastic job keeping everything neat. "Riley, it's me, Marcy!" I called from the bottom of the steps.

"Hey, Marce. Come on up!"

She was propped up in bed against a mountain of pillows. Her black hair was gleaming, and she was wearing mascara and lipstick. Her laptop and cell phone were sitting on a small table by the bed. A deposition lay on a pillow beside her, and law journals and books were also on the bed.

I smiled. "You look terrific. How are you?"

"Laura keeps kicking my spleen."

"Laura? That's pretty."

She laughed softly. "Thanks. Keith and I finally found a girl's name we could agree on—no one I'd hated in school, no one I'd prosecuted, no one he'd dated. Anyway, I'd ground her from gymnastics or dance or whatever it is she's currently engaged in, but what would I do? Send her to her womb?" At my silence, she continued. "Man! Everybody's a critic. I know it was cheesy, but I thought it was kinda cute."

"I'm sorry. It was cute. I just have a lot on my mind this morning."

"The police aren't any closer to nabbing Francesca Ortega's assailant?"

"That's not the worst of it. He's struck again." I went on to explain about Cassandra.

Riley began expressing her condolences for Frederic and for me because I'd found the body, but I interrupted.

"I need your help, Riley. I was looking through a photo album at the apartment and came across a stock certificate for the Santiago Corporation."

"Do you think that's what the killer—or Cassandra—had been looking for?"

"I'm not sure. The certificate I found has no name on it, so unless it's like a bearer bond, it wouldn't be worth much . . . would it?"

"I don't know," Riley said. "So you want me to investigate the Santiago Corporation's stocks."

"Yeah, but I'd also like you to dig as deeply into their financials as you can. When I worked at the accounting firm, we looked closely at acquisitions, mergers, research, and development expenditures when we audited—you know, to see if the company had been padding its profits."

She frowned. "Because you found a stock certificate at Francesca Ortega's apartment, you think the Santiago Corporation cooks their books?"

"I realize it's a stretch," I admitted. "But Francesca was fired for snooping. What if she took this document and hid it in her photo album in order to prove the Santiago Corporation was guilty of something involving their stock or their shareholders?"

"But from what you've told me previously, she was megaloyal to the dad, right?" Riley asked.

"Yeah." I frowned, not following her.

"Then why would she have brought the certificate home? Why wouldn't she have presented her case to Caleb Sr.?"

"Maybe she did," I said. "Maybe that's why she was fired. Do you mind seeing what you can find?"

"Not at all. But without seeing the Santiago

Corporation's actual records, it's going to be hard to prove anything."

"At this point, I don't need to prove it. I only need to see if I'm on the right track."

When I got to the shop, I started working on the ribbon embroidery purse I planned to carry to the masquerade ball. I thought it would be easy enough to finish by Saturday, and on Monday I could set up the window display.

The bells above the door jingled, and I looked up to see Todd striding in.

"Good morning," I said.

"It has to be better than the night you had," he said.

I gave him a wry smile. "You heard."

He nodded. "It was the talk of MacKenzies' Mochas this morning."

"I'm surprised Sadie isn't here yet."

"She'll probably be here after the rush." He sat down on the sofa opposite me. "So, are you okay?"

I slowly nodded. "Yeah. On the one hand, I wish I hadn't been the one to find Cassandra, but on the other, I'm glad Frederic didn't. It was such a shock to him, anyway. . . ."

"You don't sound so certain."

"I am," I said, trying to force more conviction into my voice. "Her wounds were consistent with those suffered by Francesca, and I know Frederic didn't kill his mother."

"You don't really know. I mean, you feel sorry for him, and you don't want to think him capable of the crimes," Todd said. "Just be careful around him. Don't trust him too much."

"I won't." I bit my lip. "So that's the talk at the coffeehouse this morning—that Frederic is suspected of killing Cassandra?"

"Not so much that, just that Cassandra had been found murdered." He spread his hands. "The logical suspect is Frederic."

"I know . . . I just don't think it was him." I looked at Todd. "You've met him. What do you think?"

"I don't think he's a killer, but then I'm not a psychologist."

"You tend bar," I pointed out. "Doesn't that count?"

He grinned. "I could maybe qualify as an amateur judge of character, but that's certainly not infallible. I've been wrong about plenty of people in the past."

"Tell me about it," I said.

"Speaking of tending bar, I need to get across the street," he said. "Call me if you need anything, okay?"

"I will. I might stop by to get some apricot ale to take home after class tonight. That or a bottle of chardonnay."

"Been that kind of day already?" he asked.

"It's been that kind of week."

He chuckled. "Yeah, I know. I'll see you later."

After Todd left, I decided it was time to do something I didn't really want to. I called David. He answered on the first ring.

"Hi, there," I said with a cheerfulness I definitely did not feel. "I wanted to see if you could stop by the shop sometime today."

"Why?" he asked, his tone laced with suspicion.

"Because we ended things on a bad note the other evening, and I don't want that. We meant too much to each other once to wind up enemies, don't you agree?"

"I guess." He was silent for a moment. "Wouldn't it be better for me to come by your house? That way, we wouldn't be constantly interrupted by your customers."

"I have a late class tonight." To myself, I added, *Besides, I'm afraid to be alone with you.* "How about dropping by during lunchtime? The shop is usually slower then."

"Does that mean you want me to bring lunch?" he asked, as if I were calling him to wheedle a meal out of him rather than merely asking him to stop by and chat.

"No, not unless you're hungry. I'm fine. I'll eat an energy bar sometime during the afternoon."

"Whatever."

I gritted my teeth and tried not to sound angry. I wanted to talk to David to find out what he knew about the Santiago Corporation and what—if any—shady dealings Francesca Ortega might've caught someone involved in. He might not know much, but I didn't want to talk with Frederic about it if I could get the information from David. "I'll look forward to seeing you soon, David."

"Yeah. See ya."

As soon as I ended the call, I growled. Thanks to David's snippy attitude, I didn't know if he'd show up or not.

I was relieved that a customer came in right after our conversation and that she needed help locating several skeins of embroidery floss for a project she was doing.

"This woman takes oil paintings and converts them to cross-stitch works," the woman said, showing me the photo of the completed design from the pattern book.

"Oh, wow," I breathed. "This is incredible. May I copy the Web address down from the back of your book? I'd love to carry some of her stuff here in my shop."

"Of course! I just hope I can get mine to look like hers did when it's finished." She made a face to underscore her self-doubt.

"You'll do fine. And if I can be of any assistance whatsoever, come on back and see me," I said.

I helped her find all the thread she needed, rang her up, and put my card in her bag.

Those really were lovely patterns, and the finished products looked more like oil paintings than needlecraft. As soon as the customer had left, I went into the office to log on to the Web site. I filled out the contact information, telling the company a bit about the Seven-Year Stitch and asking to become a vendor for the designs.

Afterward, I decided to do some more digging into the Santiago Corporation on my own. I trusted Riley to find out what she could, but two sets of eyes are always better than one. I did a search for the Santiago Corporation corporate information and found various FAQ. One site indicated that the company had both a retail and contract segment. The contract segment sold to government agencies, businesses, and foreign entities. I also found the most recent quarter's financial statement, but, as Riley had indicated, this wasn't the official record.

To get a broader picture of the office supply industry's current economic situation, I researched the Santiago Corporation's competition. I learned that Santiago was in third place behind OfficePro and Stockers. There used to be an old ad slogan that went "We're number two. We try harder." What would number three do to get ahead?

A couple years ago, Stockers had attempted a

takeover of the Santiago Corporation. That must have been about the time Caleb Sr. had stepped down and turned the company over to his son. The son had turned down the offer, and the company had shown tremendous growth since then. I read that Santiago had also shown a lot of initiative in economic growth since Caleb Jr. had been in charge, even hiring consultants to make their operations greener.

Could that be it? Could the Santiago Corporation have been padding their Research and Development Department expenditures in order to gain capital, making the company appear to be more solvent than it actually was? I had to wonder what inroads the business had made since hiring their environmental consultants.

Chapter Twenty

David came by the shop at twelve thirty. It wasn't hard to see that he'd tried to make me believe he wasn't coming . . . as if I'd be worried about him or hurt because he'd rebuffed my invitation. In fact, the smirk on his face irritated me to the point that I'd have asked him to leave if I didn't need whatever information he might be able to provide. So, on that thought, I smiled and said I was glad he could make it.

"I stopped for lunch at a restaurant on the other side of town," he said as he sauntered over to the sit-and-stitch square. "The waitress was cute. She wrote her phone number on a napkin and slipped it to me with my bill."

"That's good. You should give her a call." I shrugged. "That is, if you're planning to stay in the area."

David took his coat off and laid it across the arm of the sofa before sitting down. "What? I can't call her if I'm not sticking around?"

"Well, of course you could."

"Yeah, I could," he said. "Serious relationships seem to have left a bad taste in my mouth lately. Maybe I could use a little more casual fun."

"And maybe we should talk about something a little less volatile," I said, "especially since we're trying to get along. Would you like something to drink? I have sodas, water, and fruit juice in my fridge."

"No, thanks. I'm good."

"So, tell me what all you've been up to—jobwise. What did you do for the Santiago Corporation—human resources?"

"Is that what this is about?" David asked. "You asked me here to find out more about the Santiago Corporation?"

I sighed. "There's no way we can be friends and get a fresh start if you're going to take offense to everything I say."

"I'm sorry." He rubbed his chin. "You're right. I shouldn't be suspicious of everything you say. It's just that you made it clear you weren't interested in me in the least—that you were downright scared of me—and then out of the blue you call. What am I supposed to think?"

"You're supposed to think I cared too much about what we once had for us to harbor so much animosity toward each other." Okay, so I had an ulterior motive, too. I shook my head. "This was a mistake."

He sat there for a moment in silence. Then he said quietly, "I wasn't in human resources. I was an environmental consultant for the Santiago Corporation."

Bingo. "That's impressive. I didn't know you did that kind of work."

"I have an MBA. I have a number of business specialties I can draw on."

"Cool. What exactly did you do?" I asked.

"I studied the impact of deforestation, the cost of restocking forests and implementing more environmentally friendly manufacturing procedures . . . things like that." He shrugged. "I enjoyed it while it lasted."

"What happened?"

"Budget cuts—at least, that's what Junior said."

I pursed my lips. "Were you trying to talk with Caleb Sr. about getting your job back before the funeral on Tuesday?"

David nodded. "I thought if I could make him see the value of my work, he'd hire me back."

"Did you get anywhere with him?"

"He told me he'd take it up with the board at their next executive meeting," he said.

"Well, good luck."

David smiled. "Thanks. It's a good company to work for . . . I mean, it used to be."

"At dinner the other night, Caleb Sr. told me that he and his wife are separated," I said. "Is that true, or was it just a case of an old man trying to be flirtatious?"

"Are you asking because you're interested?"

I laughed. "Hardly. Only curious."

"He was telling the truth. She lives in their town house in the city, and he occupies their country home," said David.

If Caleb Sr. lived in a home he once shared with his wife, then it's possible she'd left the jewelry there. And Caleb Sr. could've given that jewelry to Francesca . . . But how would June Santiago have known it was missing and reported it stolen?

David snapped his fingers. "Earth to Marcy. Come in, Marcy."

"I'm sorry," I said. "Are they amicable—the Santiagos?"

"I don't know. Why are you so fascinated with the Santiagos?"

"Because of Francesca Ortega, I guess."

"Darling, you need to move past that," he said, a hint of exasperation in his voice.

"I'd love to," I said. "But Cassandra Wainwright was murdered last night."

His eyes widened. "Murdered? Are you sure?"

"Positive. I'm the one who found her."

He got up and moved over to the same sofa I was sitting on. He put his arm around me and pulled me close. "Where was she?"

"In Francesca's apartment."

"And you found her?"

I nodded. "Frederic had asked Harriet and me to help him go through some of his mom's things."

"He asked you and Harriet but not his fiancée?" David frowned. "That sounds fishy."

"They'd had a falling-out the night before," I said.

"Even fishier. Where was he when you found her?" he asked.

"On his way to the apartment. He and Harriet got there just minutes after I did."

"That seems convenient," David said. "Are the police investigating Frederic?"

"I'm sure they are. But, at least, I think they've eliminated me as a suspect. I have an alibi for the time of death."

"You were a suspect? Are you kidding me?"

I barked out a short laugh. "I wish. But I did find the body, you know."

"Again, I think that's awfully convenient for Frederic Ortega."

"Did you know him well . . . from when you worked with him at the Santiago Corporation?"

"No, we didn't work together very much. I don't know enough about him to determine whether or not I believe him capable of murder." He gave me a one-armed hug. "But then, do we ever really know what someone else is capable of doing?"

* * *

David barely had time to get to his car before Sadie barreled into the Seven-Year Stitch.

"Was that David I saw leaving?" she asked. "What was he doing here? Did you kick him out?"

"Slow down and take a breath," I instructed with a grin. "He was here because I called and invited him."

Sadie rolled her eyes and came over to press her palm against my forehead. "Are you sick?"

"No . . . but I might be a bit calculating," I said as Sadie sat down. I explained to Sadie that I'd run across a stock certificate at Francesca Ortega's apartment after finding Cassandra. "Since David had worked for the Santiago Corporation, I thought he might be able to give me a little insight into the company."

"And did he?"

"Some. I didn't come right out and ask him the questions I'd have liked to, because I'm not convinced I can trust David."

"Ya think?" Sadie asked. "Sorry. That kinda slipped out."

"It's okay. Anyway, I got a few new pieces of the puzzle that I can pass along to Ted," I said. "And Riley is helping me dig into the Santiago Corporation's financials."

She nodded toward the ribbon-rose-bedecked fabric on my lap. "What's that?"

"It's a purse I'm making to go with the dress I'm wearing to the masquerade ball. I made Vera one and decided to make myself one, too. After the ball, I can use it in a window display and to try to create some interest in a class this spring."

"It looks hard," she said.

"It isn't. Watch." I wove the ribbon through the spokes of the spiderweb to create a rose.

Sadie smiled. "That's all there is to it?"

"That's it. You just need to be patient and not tug on the ribbon too hard or too quickly."

"I want to learn. If you offer a class, sign me up." She watched with unveiled excitement as I made another rose. "I mean it. Sign me up!"

"I can teach you how to make a rose now, if you want."

"I'd better not," Sadie said. "I need to get back to the coffeehouse. We've been busier than usual today." She cocked her head. "By the way, have you taken your Kuba cloth quilt to Lincoln City yet?"

"No. I'm planning to take it tomorrow after work."

"Want me to tag along?" she asked.

It was the nonchalance she'd forced into her voice that made me question her motives. "Do you need something from Lincoln City? Or are you afraid I'll stumble upon another dead body while I'm there?"

"A little of both. I'd like to check out the festival

setup . . . and I'd like to be there in case . . . you know . . . anything weird happens."

"You're welcome to ride along," I said with a wry grin, "as long as you don't feel like you have to."

"Trust me. You'll be doing me a favor. Blake, Todd, and some of their friends are getting together to play poker tomorrow night."

I brightened. "All right, then. On the way back, we can stop somewhere for dinner."

Sadie gave me a thumbs-up. "Oh yeah. A road trip combined with girls' night out. Does it get any better?"

Business was brisk after Sadie left, and I didn't have time to call Riley until nearly four thirty.

"It appears you made a good guess with regard to the Santiago Corporation funneling a boatload of cash into research and development and their stocks going up in value," she said. "On the other hand, there was nothing that immediately sends up red flags."

"So, at least on paper, everything looks fine for the Santiago Corporation," I said.

"It looks great. Either Junior or the people advising him are doing an excellent job of making his business dealings appear legitimate—that is, assuming they're not."

"Like I told you this morning," I reminded Riley, "at this point I'm not trying to prove anything. I'm hoping to smoke out a killer."

"Promise me you won't go off half-cocked, making a bunch of unfounded accusations."

"How about if I go off fully cocked?" I asked.

"Marcy!"

I laughed. "I'm kidding!" And I was . . . for the most part.

"You'd better be. Laura is going to need a lot more cute embroidered stuff after she arrives."

"I know."

After talking with Riley, I straightened up the shop and fluffed the sofa pillows for the evening class. I was on my way out the door to go home and feed Angus when my cell phone rang. It was Agent Daltrey. He wanted to meet with me either this evening or first thing tomorrow morning. I asked him to come by the shop after my class. No sense dreading our little get-together all night long.

Chapter Twenty-one

Agent Daltrey came into the Seven-Year Stitch less than five minutes after my last student left. It made me feel as if he'd been watching the shop, although he did act surprised when Angus loped over to greet him. After having left the poor baby at home this morning, I wanted to have him with me this evening.

"Hello, big fella," Agent Daltrey said, holding out the back of his hand for the dog to sniff. "What's his name?"

"Angus," I answered. "Would you like something to drink, Agent Daltrey?"

"I'd love some water if you have it, and please call me Jason."

I went to my office and got four bottles of water. "I hope you don't mind," I said, "but I asked detectives Nash and Sloan to join us. They should be here any minute."

"I don't mind in the least," Jason said. "In fact, I'm glad we'll all be able to sit down and put our heads together on this one."

I smiled as I handed him his water. "I'm happy you feel that way." I sat down and twisted the top off my bottle.

Ted and Harriet arrived, and Ted took on Angus in a quick game of tug-of-war before we got down to business. Harriet sat with me on the sofa facing the window, and the men sat opposite us.

"So, what're we doing?" Ted asked.

"I called Marcy to ask her for more information about the crime scene she happened upon yesterday," Jason said.

"You've undoubtedly read the report I gave to the county deputies?" I asked.

"I have," he said. "But I must say, respectfully, that I might be able to glean more from talking with you than I did from scanning their notes."

"That makes sense." I described entering the apartment, going through the various rooms, and then finding Cassandra in Francesca's home office. "The room was a wreck. Papers were thrown all over the place, drawers were open . . . I thought someone had been trying desperately to find something."

"You didn't feel the crime scene had been staged?" Jason asked.

"No," I said. "Did you?"

"I don't know. When I looked at the crime scene photos earlier today, I wondered if Ms. Wainwright had trashed the room in a rage prior to her murder or whether the killer had taken the time to toss the room after dispensing with her." Jason took a drink of his water. "Being that you were the first to arrive on the scene, what was your initial impression?"

I shrugged. "My thought was that either Cassandra surprised the killer as he was riffling through the room or he stabbed her before searching the office."

"And, Detective Sloan, what did you perceive?" Jason asked.

"I saw no blood on the papers, the desk, the file cabinet . . . none of the places the murderer would have touched while trashing the office," said Harriet. "So either he or she searched first and killed later or Cassandra Wainwright was the person who'd been looking for something."

Jason raised his bottle. "Hear, hear! We need to determine what Francesca Ortega had that was of value to Ms. Wainwright, to the killer, or to them both."

"There is one thing that happened after I gave my statement to the county officers," I said. I told them about the stock certificate falling out of the photo album and my suspicion that Francesca might've caught someone at the Santiago Corporation padding stocks.

"I don't follow," Ted said.

"Okay," I said, taking a deep breath and wondering how to best explain my mind-set. "Since the certificate had no name on it, I believe Francesca might've taken it more for symbolic rather than lucrative reasons. Maybe she'd planned to show—or had actually shown—the certificate to someone higher up in the company to get them to investigate the books."

"You believe Francesca Ortega learned that someone within the corporation was keeping fraudulent records," Ted said.

"I feel that's a strong possibility. You see, when I worked as an auditor, we'd look for lots of money being earmarked for R and D—research and development—because it's easy to use that designation as a place to cover up hokey transactions."

"Where's the certificate now?" Jason asked.

"I put it back in the photo album," I said.

Ted leaned forward, placing his forearms on his knees. "Who do you think knew about the fraud if the company was indeed falsifying records?"

"The person responsible, of course," I said, "as well as anyone helping to funnel the money." I tilted my head. "I did learn something else interesting today. Until a few weeks ago, David Frist was working in the Santiago Corporation's R and D department as an environmental consultant."

Jason asked, "Who's David Frist?"

"An old . . . friend of mine from San Francisco. He came by the shop the day before Francesca was stabbed."

"And he got here pretty quickly on the morning of her death," Ted supplied.

"Do you feel this man was involved in Ms. Ortega's and Ms. Wainwright's murders?" Jason was taking notes on a small pad he'd taken from his jacket pocket and didn't look up.

"I have no idea," I admitted. "I'm only spitballing."

"What about the jewelry?" Harriet asked Jason. "Do you have any new leads there?"

"Not any new ones, no."

"Do you know where Mrs. Santiago kept these particular pieces?" I asked.

Jason shook his head. "Why do you ask?"

"I'm just wondering if they might've been at the summer home," I said. "Since Mr. and Mrs. Santiago have been estranged for quite some time, someone could've taken the jewelry from there believing Mrs. Santiago wouldn't realize it was missing."

"Even at that," Jason said, "how would it wind up with Francesca Ortega unless she stole it?"

"That's what we need to figure out," I said.

When I got home, I took out my cell phone and found the incoming number Caleb Santiago Sr.

had used to call me last week. My number must have appeared on his caller identification screen, because he answered, "Hello, Ms. Singer."

"Hi, Mr. Santiago. I wanted to call and thank you again for dinner the other evening."

"You're quite welcome," he said. "Now tell me the real reason for your call."

I chuckled. "And you accused me of cutting directly to the chase." I cleared my throat. "You told me you and your wife are separated."

"That's correct."

"I'm sorry, but I have to ask. I mean, you're an attractive man . . . Francesca was a lovely woman. Was there more to your relationship than typical employer-employee status?"

"We'd worked together for more than twenty years, Ms. Singer. Naturally, that would upgrade us to acquaintances at the very least, wouldn't it?"

"Not necessarily," I said. "I've known people who've worked for a company for a long time but haven't spoken with a boss other than their immediate supervisor."

"I was Frannie's immediate supervisor."

"Were you having an affair with her, Mr. Santiago?"

"Why do you ask?"

"I'm thinking maybe you gave Francesca some of the jewelry your wife had at your summer home," I said. "When Mrs. Santiago came looking for it, she decided it must have been stolen. And maybe you simply had Francesca break the pieces up so that she wouldn't be prosecuted if she was found with the jewels in her possession."

"You have quite an imagination," Mr. Santiago said. "But Frannie and I weren't having an affair. My tastes tend to run toward younger women. That said, the next time I find myself in your area, I'll give you a call."

Yikes. Not knowing quite how to answer that, I replied, "Okay. Thank you for your time, Mr. Santiago."

After ending the call, I realized Mr. Santiago hadn't denied my theory about how Francesca came into possession of the jewelry. He had only denied the affair.

The next morning, I was ensconced in a chair in the sit-and-stitch square finishing my ribbon embroidery purse, with Angus snoozing in his bed beneath the counter, when Frederic came by. He dropped onto the sofa with a dramatic sigh.

I started to ask him what was wrong, but that seemed like a stupid question in light of everything life had thrown at Frederic over the past few days. Instead, I asked, "Is there anything I can do?"

"What was Agent Daltrey doing here last night?"

"He came by with some questions about the

crime scene . . . at your mother's apartment," I said. "I knew he was coming, so I asked Ted and Harriet to be here. Something about that guy makes me nervous."

"Tell me about it." He bit his thumbnail, which was already nibbled nearly to the quick. "He thinks I did it, doesn't he?"

"He didn't give me any indication of that." Of course, he didn't let on that he believed Frederic to be innocent, either, but I didn't tell Frederic that. "He and Harriet did point out something I hadn't considered. There was no blood on any of the papers or the desk or anything."

"So? Why's that important?" Frederic asked.

"Either it means the killer was riffling through the office and was surprised by Cassandra, stabbed her, and then ran away, or it means Cassandra was the one looking for something." There was the other possibility that the two of them were working together, but I kept that one to myself. "Is there anything Cassandra might have been searching for at your mom's place?"

"I have no idea . . . unless it was her Santiago stock."

My eyes widened. "Your mom kept her stock at her house?"

"Yeah. That's how little they're worth," he said. "When Caleb Sr. stepped down as CEO, he gave Mom a hundred shares of stock. They're currently worth five dollars a share."

"Were these shares made out to her, or were they like bearer bonds?" I asked.

"They were like bearer bonds. That way, if anything happened to her, they'd pass directly to me." He rotated one index finger in the air. "Five hundred dollars' worth of stock—*woo-hoo.*"

"At the apartment the other night while you were talking with the deputies, I looked through the photo album on the coffee table. A stock certificate fell out onto my lap. I put it back in the book, but I did notice there wasn't a name on it."

"You should've taken it. It would have netted you five big ones . . . unless the stock has dropped again within the past few days."

"So the stock isn't doing well?" I asked.

He shook his head. "That was a crappy thing for an employer who said my mom was like family to him to do, don't you think? Give her five hundred shares of almost worthless stock instead of a pension?"

"That—the stock—was in lieu of her pension?"

"Yep," Frederic said. "Good old Santiago Corporation. Always looking out for the little people."

"Do you think it's possible Caleb Sr. gave your mother the jewelry?"

He frowned. "Why would he do that?"

I shrugged. "Maybe he felt bad about the crappy stock." I set the embroidery work aside and leaned forward. "Think about it. His wife wasn't living with him. He was at the summer house, and she was at the town house. Maybe she'd left behind this expensive jewelry, and Caleb Sr. gave it to your mom to thank her for years of service."

"Why not give her a monetary bonus?"

"Bonuses show up on the books. Jewelry doesn't," I said. "Then, what if Mrs. Santiago decided she wanted to wear her sapphire necklace somewhere and sent somebody over to the summer house to get it? When the person came back empty-handed, she could've confronted her husband, who said the jewelry must have been stolen. She then reported the theft. Isn't it possible Caleb Sr. could've called your mom at that point to have her take the pieces apart and sell them?"

"It's possible," Frederic said. "Only Mom didn't sell them. She wanted you to put them on Cass's gown."

"Maybe after the wedding, she was going to tell you guys the truth about the jewels."

"Possibly." He leaned back against the sofa and closed his eyes. "I just wish she'd told me all this before."

"Well, it's mostly speculation on my part," I said, "although it is a good explanation of how your mother gained possession of some of Mrs. Santiago's jewelry."

He opened his eyes and sat up. "You could be right. Unfortunately, we'll probably never know."

"I'm sorry."

"Me, too." He stood and slipped his coat back on.

I repeated my overused sentiment to let me know if he needed anything. After he left, I resumed work on my purse. All I had left to do was add the leaves, some seed pearls and some crystal beads. And sew the back and straps on, of course. But that would be easy. I felt confident I'd be finished with the purse before I left the shop this evening.

My thoughts kept returning to Frederic. He'd suffered so much tragedy here in Tallulah Falls. I wondered if after everything was dispensed with in regard to his mother's estate and Cassandra's funeral, he'd leave here and go someplace to start fresh . . . leave all these hurtful memories behind him.

I remembered him saying that Agent Daltrey believed he was guilty. He'd been awfully anxious to find out why Agent Daltrey was here yesterday evening. Of course, I would be, too, if I were in Frederic's position. Wouldn't I?

Ted was right. I didn't really know Frederic or his mother. Maybe they had conspired to steal the jewels. Maybe Frederic's devotion to Francesca was an act. Maybe he'd dated Cassandra in order to get legal insights. Maybe he'd killed both women because they were mere obstacles to overcome.

I shuddered. I needed to quit letting my imagination get the best of me. Frederic was a good guy. I could feel it. He loved his mother, and even though he didn't feel he and Cassandra were right for each other anymore, he had loved her, too. He wasn't a violent person. He was kind.

I worked on my leaves and hummed a little tune to try to avoid letting my thoughts run amok. After all, none of us even knew that Francesca's and Cassandra's deaths weren't random acts . . . robberies gone wrong. Who was I kidding? There was nothing random about those murders.

I hummed louder.

Chapter Twenty-two

After closing up the shop that afternoon, I took Angus home for dinner. Sadie rode with us so we could go straight on to Lincoln City. I unlocked the door, and Angus bounded inside to wait in the kitchen by his bowl. Sadie laughed as I hurried behind the big lug to fill his bowl with kibble. I noticed the answering machine light blinking and played the message.

"Marcy, hi, it's David. Thought maybe if you weren't busy this evening, we could get together. *Um* . . . give me a call if you get this and want to do something."

Sadie huffed. "What does it take for that guy to get the hint that you're not interested?"

"I don't know. He could just be . . . you know, trying to be nice."

"Are you really that gullible?" Sadie asked.

"The nice thing could be mostly my fault," I said.

"How do you figure?"

"Well . . . when I wanted to find out what he knew about the Santiago Corporation, I kinda told him we meant too much to each other in the past to have such animosity between us now," I said. "I really pushed the friendship angle."

Sadie sighed. "I just hope that doesn't come back to bite you in the butt."

"Me, too."

After Angus had finished eating, I let him out into the backyard. I turned to Sadie. "Ready?"

"Yep. Got the quilt?"

"Oh yeah. I only hope it goes over well," I said.

"It will, Marce. It's gorgeous."

I grinned. "Thanks."

We got into the Jeep and headed in the direction of Lincoln City.

"I'm getting excited about the ball," I said.

"So am I. Has Ted mentioned what sort of costume he'll be wearing?"

"No." I frowned. "I figured he'd wear a suit and a mask. I mean, I'm not going as a particular character. Are you?"

"Not really, but before I decided on the more Victorian masquerade costume I'm wearing, I researched the Venetian carnival characters."

"That figures," I said with a smile. "You always did like to go all out."

"Well, if you're going to do something, do it right. Anyway, I can see Ted as Captain Scaramouche, the young swashbuckling adventurer."

I laughed. "Really? I can't. I can see him as Ted wearing a suit and a mask. Tell me more about the Venetians."

"Well, there's Colombina," she said. "That means 'little dove' in Italian. She's a comic servant. And there's Arlecchino, the most popular of the comic servants whose specialty is his physical agility. Brighella is Arlecchino's moneygrubbing, wicked older brother." She tilted her head up while she thought. "Oh, and there's this guy called Burrattino who looks like Pinocchio, and Dottore Peste, the plague doctor, who has this really long beak that was supposed to help keep him from catching the plague."

"Sounds charming," I said, eyebrows raised.

"Well, I guess you'd have to be there. I really wanted a Dama mask, but the ones I liked were too expensive."

"What's a Dama mask?" I asked.

"They're traditional women's Venetian masks. They're full-face masks with ornate headpieces that feature paintings from Carnival or patterns and jewels. They're incredible."

"They sound beautiful."

We arrived in Lincoln City and pulled into a parking space near the Rocking Horse Antique Mall. We got out of the car and I took the bagged quilt out of the back seat before locking up. It was cold, and I was glad I'd worn a heavier coat than usual.

"What's our first stop?" Sadie asked.

"I'm going into this little boutique between the Kelp Bed and Carousel By the Sea Antiques. See it?" I pointed. "It's called Yesteryear Textiles, but everything in the store doesn't have to be an antique. It can simply be based on older designs."

"Cool." She looked around. "What's with all the red bottles and redhead references?"

"I'm not sure, but it seems to be getting a lot of attention. We'll ask Jenny when we get to Yesteryear. This might give Todd some ideas for promotion, don't you think?"

"Yeah," Sadie said, "and Blake and me, too."

"Has Todd mentioned who he's taking to the ball?" I asked, trying to keep things nonchalant.

"No, why? Are you wishing he'd asked you before Ted did?"

"No. I'm happy to be going with Ted. I just . . ." I shrugged. "I just wondered."

We went into Yesteryear Textiles, and Jenny bragged on the quilt.

"I'll be happy to display the quilt," she said. "Did you bring some cards or flyers for the Seven-Year Stitch?"

"I brought both." I took the envelope containing the flyers for classes and my business cards out of my huge yellow purse and handed it to Jenny. "Thank you so much for doing this."

"Are you willing to sell the quilt?" Jenny asked.

I looked at Sadie and then back at Jenny. "I really want it to get some attention for the store."

Jenny cocked her head. "What if someone wants to buy the quilt and then pick it up the last day of the festival?"

"Would anyone be willing to do that?" I asked.

She nodded. "We do it every year."

"Great. Then you're welcome to sell it for whatever you think it's worth," I said.

Jenny laughed. "Oh no, you don't. Set your price."

"Two hundred?" I asked.

"That's a little cheap," she said, "but it should sell quickly for that amount. Heck, I might even buy it myself."

"Thank you, Jenny," I said.

"By the way," Sadie said, "what's the deal with the red bottles?"

"We're honoring redheads past and present this year," Jenny said with a grin. "As an old gray-haired lady, I don't qualify."

"You're far from old," I said, "and neither Sadie nor I qualify, either."

"You can still vote for your favorite celeb redhead, though," Jenny said.

"Conan," Sadie said.

"Lucy," I said simultaneously.

We all shared a laugh, and then Sadie and I said good-bye. I told Jenny I'd check in with her about the quilt sometime next week.

Sadie and I stepped out of the cozy shop and back onto the cold, bustling street.

A man's voice stopped me in my tracks. "Well, hello."

"David. What are you doing here?"

He shrugged. "I'm just enjoying all the preparations for Antique Week. It should be a blast, don't you think?"

"Yeah," I said. "It—it looks fun."

"Are you guys planning to come back next week?" he asked.

"Maybe," I said.

"So, would you two like to join me for dinner?" David spread his hands. "I'm buying, of course."

"No, thank you," Sadie said. "We have plans."

"We do," I said. "But thank you, anyway."

"Sure. Some other time, then." David turned and watched us go. I could feel his eyes boring into my back as Sadie and I hurried to the Jeep.

"How about instead of stopping somewhere for dinner, we go back to my house?" I suggested. "I'll cook."

"We can cook together," Sadie said. "Anything to avoid having that creep follow us to a restaurant. I can't believe he's still stalking you after Ted confronted him at the lodge."

"I guess it could've been a coincidence," I said.

"Yeah, as much as you or I could win the favorite redhead contest."

I inclined my head. "You've got a point. Let's just go home and have dinner. I even have a lasagna in the freezer, so all we'll have to do is let that bake."

"Run me by the café, and I'll pick us up some brownies." Sadie smiled. "While we're waiting for the lasagna to bake, we'll nosh on brownies and watch corny old game shows."

After making a quick stop at MacKenzies' Mochas, Sadie and I went to my house. I preheated the oven while she warmed the brownies in the microwave. We opted not to bring Angus in until we'd put the brownies away. He could have a small plate of lasagna, but he couldn't have a brownie.

As Sadie went into the living room and turned on the game show channel, my phone rang. I answered it, but I didn't recognize the voice.

"Is this Marcy?" the caller asked.

"Yes, it is. Who's this?"

"It's Caleb Santiago Jr. I'd like to meet with you to clear up these misunderstandings you seem to have about Francesca and my father. Can you meet me in Toledo tomorrow?"

"I'm afraid I can't, Mr. Santiago. I'm busy all day tomorrow," I said. "But, please, rest assured. I'm not accusing your father of anything. Whatever kind of relationship he and Francesca Ortega had, I'm sure it wasn't inappropriate." Okay, I wasn't really sure. I just wanted to get this guy off the phone. I could hear *Family Feud* playing in the living room.

"I still would like to talk with you," he said. "Are you sure you can't change your plans around and meet me at the lodge in Toledo?"

"I'm positive. I'm working until five o'clock; and after that, I'm going to a masquerade ball sponsored by our Chamber of Commerce."

"I see. Well, could I maybe come by your shop sometime tomorrow and talk with you then?" he asked.

"Sure," I said. "That'll be fine."

"Great. I look forward to seeing you then. Have a good night, Marcy."

"You, too, Mr. Santiago."

I ended the call and went into the living room, where Sadie was waiting. "That was Caleb Santiago Jr. He wants to come by the shop tomorrow and talk with me about his dad and Francesca Ortega."

She wrinkled her brow. "Why?"

"Well . . . I kinda called his dad and asked if he was having an affair with Francesca and if he'd given her some of his estranged wife's jewelry."

Sadie's jaw dropped. "Marcy! Are you nuts?"

"I wanted to know," I said.

She ran both hands through her hair. "Subtlety is not one of your virtues, is it?"

"I guess not," I said.

"You think he'll sue you for defamation of character or something?" she asked.

"No. He can't. I didn't accuse anyone of anything. I didn't say something like, 'Hey, I know you were sleeping with Francesca.' I merely asked the man if he'd had an affair with the woman. That can't be considered defamatory."

"Just be careful," she said. "The son is probably royally ticked off because he thinks you're dragging his family name through the mud."

Chapter Twenty-three

When Angus and I went into the shop Saturday morning, I was pretty excited. I was really looking forward to the ball, which was kind of odd because I hadn't even wanted to go when I'd first heard about it.

Vera burst into the shop at around eleven almost in tears.

"Vera, what's wrong?" I asked. "I thought you'd be even more excited about tonight than I am."

"I am excited about tonight," she said. "It's right now that has me about to scream and pull my hair out."

"What happened?"

She came over to join me in the sit-and-stitch square. "Look." She handed me her needlepoint project. "It's ruined."

I examined the piece. "Where? I don't see anything wrong with it."

"I missed a stitch right here." She pointed to an area of the cloth, but I still didn't see anything wrong.

"It looks fine, Vera. Trust me; you're the only one who'll ever know."

"But I'll know!" she wailed. "I started to rip out everything I've done since I missed the stitch, but I just didn't have the heart. Will you do it?"

I got up. "Come with me." I led Vera over to a framed needlepoint piece I'd done of a fairy. Angus followed us and looked up expectantly. I took the piece down and handed it to Vera. "Pick out the mistake in this."

Vera scrutinized the fairy, turning the frame first one way and then another. "You're putting me on. There is no mistake in this piece. It's beautiful."

"Thank you. But there is a mistake in it . . . more than one, to be precise." I pointed to a portion of the fairy's multicolored dress. "I missed more than one stitch here and had to adjust other stitches to compensate."

"You're kidding."

I shook my head. "I'm not. But I—and now you—am the only one who knows that. Just like you and I are the only ones who know about your mistake," I said with a gentle smile. "Finish the piece, Vera. It'll look terrific."

She grinned. "You really think so?"

"I know so."

We returned to the sit-and-stitch square, where she resumed work on her project, and I finished up the purse I was taking to the ball tonight. The bells over the door heralded the arrival of Ted. He was off today and was wearing jeans, a sweat-shirt, and a black bomber jacket. He looked so yummy that my heart did a little flip.

"Hi," I said with a smile. "I didn't expect to see you so early in the day."

"I just came by to ask what color your dress is," he said, patting Angus' head. He nodded at Vera. "Hi, Ms. Langhorne."

"Hello, Ted." She packed up her tote bag. "I'll get out of your way but will see you both this evening. Thanks for everything, Marcy!"

"You're welcome."

Ted sat beside me on the sofa and dropped a quick kiss on my cheek. "So, what color is it?"

"It's ivory," I said. "Like these roses here."

"You wouldn't happen to have a scrap of that ribbon left over, would you?"

"I do." I went and got Ted about an inch of the ribbon. "What're you gonna do with that? If you're thinking cummerbund, I might have to roll off a little more."

"Oh, really? You calling me fat?"

I laughed. "Hardly. But you couldn't get that piece around a pencil."

"I just need to know about what color your dress is," he said. "And that's all you need to know."

"I had an interesting evening yesterday," I said.

"Are you planning on baiting me the entire time I'm here?"

I smiled. "Maybe."

He toyed with a strand of my hair. "Flirt."

I giggled. "Okay. Let me tell you about yesterday. Sadie and I went to Lincoln City, where they're setting everything up for the Antique Week festival. While we were walking along, we ran into David Frist."

Ted froze. "Did he accost you in any way?"

"No. He acted as if it was a coincidence that we ran into each other. Sadie didn't buy it, and I really didn't, either. But we didn't hear from him the rest of the night," I said. "I did hear from Caleb Santiago Jr., though."

"What did he want?"

"He wanted me to quit calling and asking his dad questions about Francesca Ortega and his mother's stolen jewelry," I said.

"What kind of questions are you calling and asking his dad?"

"Well . . . I asked Caleb Sr. if he and Francesca had been having an affair and if he'd given the jewelry to her prior to his estranged wife noticing they were missing. He said no and that he liked younger women."

Ted shook his head. "What am I gonna do with you, Inch-High?"

I smiled. "Dance with me."

"I will. Just please try to stay out of trouble until then, won't you?"

"I'll do my best."

"I have to go." He stood. "I have a few things to take care of before this evening. I'm looking forward to this."

"So am I."

After Ted left, I went into my office and quickly finished the rest of the purse on the sewing machine. The back was plain ivory linen, and the straps were silver cording. I was very pleased with how it had turned out.

I was still admiring my work when the bells over the door alerted me that someone had come into the shop. I set the purse down and went to attend to my customer.

The customer turned out to be a man. He was young, with black, wavy hair and an athletic build. He looked vaguely familiar.

"Hi. Welcome to the Seven-Year Stitch. How can I help you?"

"Marcy?" he asked.

"Yes."

He held out a hand. "Nicholas Santiago."

"Of course! We met at the lodge," I said, as I shook his hand. "I take it your brother or your dad sent you?"

"Yeah, Caleb sent me." He chuckled. "Junior—my brother, I mean—said he was supposed to come by here and talk with you today, but he's going to be tied up in business meetings in Toledo all day." He jerked his head toward Angus. "I don't think your dog likes me."

I frowned. "That's odd. He likes everybody." I glanced toward Angus, who was lying near my feet watching Nicholas Santiago warily. There must be something strange about this guy for Angus not to warm up to him.

He shrugged. "Nice store you've got here."

"Thank you."

"That macramé planter in the back reminds me of all the square knots I had to tie when I was in the navy."

"Where were you stationed?" I asked.

"Jacksonville, Florida," he said.

"Did you like it?" I knew from seeing the *About Us* on the company's Web site that Nicholas was now heavily involved in the family business.

"It grew me up. That's what it was supposed to do, I guess."

"Please tell your brother I'm sorry if my phone call upset your father," I said. "It certainly wasn't my intention. I just couldn't—can't—figure out for the life of me how Francesca Ortega got hold of your mother's jewels."

"She must've been craftier than any of us ever thought," he said. "It's no big deal to me. It makes sense that you'd think maybe she was fooling around with Dad and he gave them to her. I mean, he and Mom haven't lived together for a few years now."

"I'm glad you see it that way. I don't think your brother and your dad do, though."

He laughed. "Nah. Dad didn't mind all that much. I think he was just disappointed that you hadn't called him to express an interest in seeing him again. Caleb is always worried about the business—what people will think, what impression they'll have, how that will affect stocks or the company's performance . . . that kind of stuff."

"That's to be expected. He has a lot of responsibility to shoulder."

"He does. I help out where I can," he said, "but Caleb is the brains behind the business." He took a step closer to me, and Angus growled and showed his teeth.

"Angus!" I admonished.

"Whoa," Nicholas said, backing away. "Watch it there, buddy. I don't want to have to tangle with you." He moved closer to the door. "How about I just tell Caleb everything is square now and that you don't really care about Francesca Ortega and the jewels at all?"

"Suits me," I said. "I really do like your family and wouldn't do anything to hurt the business." I smiled. "Tell your dad if I was a few years older, I might be interested."

He laughed. "If you were a few years older, he wouldn't be."

Even after he left, Angus continued to growl. I was beginning to wonder if there was something else wrong with Angus when Sadie came in.

"Hi, guys!" she said.

Angus got up and trotted over to be petted by Sadie.

"Does he seem all right to you?" I asked.

"Sure. Why?"

I explained about Nicholas Santiago being here and Angus going all Cujo on him. "He even growled for a few minutes after the man left, Sadie. It kind of freaked me out. I mean, Angus has always been protective, but he's usually fine with the people who come into the shop."

"True," she said. "But usually the only men who come in here by themselves are men you know. The others are usually with women. Maybe the fact that this guy was alone seemed threatening to Angus. Or maybe he had on some weird cologne. Did he smell funny?"

"No. But he could've had a dog. . . ."

"I bet that's it." She scratched Angus behind both ears. "Did the baby smell some big mean dog on that old guy? *Huh?* Did he? Poor baby! We won't let him come back here anymore. No, we won't."

"Are you psyched about the ball?" I asked.

"Totally. Are you?"

"Yes. Ted came in earlier and asked what color my dress was. What do you think that was about?"

She straightened. "Flowers—has to be. He must be going to get you a corsage or something." She smiled. "How sweet. Oh, by the way, I found out who Todd's taking to the ball. She's a waitress who works for us."

"Oh." I didn't want to ask how cute she was or what she was like. Really, I didn't. "Is she cute?"

"She's adorable. Not as pretty as you, but cute," Sadie said.

"Good," I said. "That he's going with her, I mean."

"I knew what you meant."

I nodded.

When I got home after work, I was nearly giddy with anticipation. I fed Angus, munched on an energy bar while he ate, and then let him out into the yard. I hurried upstairs, took a quick bath, and then sat before my vanity in my robe to put on my makeup.

Even though I'd be wearing a mask much of the evening, I wanted my makeup to be perfect. One of the perks of having a mom in the Hollywood costume business is that you get to meet lots of makeup and wardrobe people as you're growing up. I'd learned makeup tips from some of the best.

When I was satisfied with my makeup, I took off the robe and slipped into the gorgeous beaded ivory gown and strappy sandals. I couldn't help smiling at my reflection. I felt just like a princess!

The doorbell rang. I grabbed my mask and purse and all but floated down the stairs. I peeped out to make sure it was, in fact, Ted, and then I opened the door.

"Wow," he said. "Just . . . wow."

I laughed. "You're pretty wow yourself." He was wearing a black suit with a white tuxedo shirt and bow tie. He was holding his mask at his side.

He handed me a white calla lily wrapped in ivory ribbon.

"Thank you," I said. "It's lovely."

"Are you ready to go?" he asked.

"I am if you are."

He smiled. "I'm ready to show you off to all of Tallulah Falls."

He escorted me to his car and held the passenger-side door open as I slid inside. As he was driving toward the convention hall, I noticed he kept looking into the rearview mirror.

"Is anything wrong?" I asked.

He shook his head. "No. Everything's great."

Still, he kept watching the rearview.

"Then why are you constantly seeing where we've been rather than where we're going?"

He frowned slightly. "I get the feeling we're being tailed."

"Maybe we are. Half the town is going to this ball," I said.

"I know. It's just . . . you mentioned David Frist followed you and Sadie to Lincoln City last night—"

"I didn't say he followed us," I interrupted. "I said we ran into him there."

"Well, there's a good chance he wants to run into you again tonight . . . coincidentally, of course." He glanced sideways at me.

"You're right. It pays to be cautious. But he can't get in, Ted. The event is invitation only."

"I know. But if there's any way around that, he'll find it."

We arrived at the ball. There was valet parking, so Ted handed over his keys, we put on our masks, and went into the ball. Still, Ted kept looking over his shoulder.

"I'm going to speak with the doorman about security," he said. "I'll make sure there's no way Frist is getting in here tonight. I'll be right back."

"All right. Ooh, I see Vera. I'm going over to say hi."

He chuckled. "I'll be there in a minute."

"Look at us," I squealed to Vera.

She laughed. "I know! We're the cat's pajamas, the bee's knees, the lion's mane . . ."

I joined in her laughter. "Have you seen Blake and Sadie?"

"Not yet," she said. "Or, then again, I might have. It's hard to tell who's who tonight."

She was right. The hall was filled with colorful people—some garish, some more subdued—most wearing masks of various kinds. Many wore full-face masks. Others, like Vera, Ted, and me, wore the masks that covered only our eyes. Mine and Vera's provided an ornate headdress as well. Some held masks on sticks, and the rest eschewed masks in favor of face paint. Even the members of the orchestra were dressed as Victorian nobles.

"This is one of the coolest parties I've ever been to," I said.

"Me, too." She opened her purse and took out a camera. "Let me get a photo of you."

"Oh, let's have someone take one of us together," I said. I looked around hoping Ted was on his way back already, but I didn't see him.

A man in a full-face Volto mask came to our aid. "Hi, Marcy. Want me to take a picture of you two?"

"Please," I said. "Who is that in there?"

He chuckled. "Who do you think?"

"Blake," Vera said. "You can't fool me."

He laughed again. "Never. Marcy, get over there beside her and both of you smile pretty."

I got beside Vera and Blake took our picture.

He handed the camera back to Vera. "I want a copy."

"Where's Sadie," I asked.

He lowered his voice. "Bathroom. She's having some sort of crisis. Will you come see if you can help?"

"Of course," I said. "Vera, tell Ted where I've gone and that I'll be back in a jiff." I turned back to Blake. "Is it the dress? She didn't get a rip in it or anything, did she?"

"Nah, I don't think it's all that serious. You'll be able to talk her down from the ledge." He took my arm and directed me through the crowd. We weaved in and out of groups and couples until we reached a hallway. "Right down here."

"Are you sure?" I asked. "It's kinda dark."

"I'm positive."

"Marcy!"

I whirled around at the sound of Blake's voice. It was Blake, all right. He was only wearing a half mask, and it was plain to see that the Blake at the far end of the hall was the real one. But if he was Blake, then who was this other Blake? I glanced back at Faux Blake to see that he'd pulled a small dagger out of his cloak. I screamed. Real Blake came barreling down the hall and tackled Faux Blake. Vera was tottering along behind Real Blake. I hurried to her side.

"Nine-one-one!" I yelled in the direction of the crowd. "Emergency!"

Faux Blake and Real Blake scrambled to their feet. Thankfully, the knife had been dislodged from Faux Blake's hand. Unfortunately, he was a pretty good fighter without it. He smashed his fist into Real Blake's nose. I screamed.

"Tallulah Falls Police," Ted shouted. "Nobody move." He stepped between Vera and me, his gun on Faux Blake. He moved closer to them and pulled the mask off Faux Blake's face. It was Nicholas Santiago.

Epilogue

So, my first masquerade ball lasted about ten minutes—twenty or so, if you count all the "excitement" with Nicholas Santiago . . . which I don't count, thank you very much. Oh well, there's always next time.

After we gave our statements to the Tallulah Falls officers on duty, Ted took me to Captain Moe's, where we played songs on the jukebox and danced the night away. Captain Moe even cut in for a couple dances.

Nicholas had been his older brother's enforcer. That meant both brothers would likely be going to prison for a long time. Francesca had caught Caleb Jr. doing some very imaginative bookkeeping. She'd taken up the matter with Caleb Sr., but he was loyal to his son. Caleb Jr. had fired Francesca and had given her the worthless stock, believing she'd think she was sitting on a gold mine. Smarter than he'd given her credit for being, Francesca investigated the stocks and found them to be junk. She contacted Junior and threatened to turn him over to the SEC. He'd used the jewels to try to keep her quiet. After his mother reported the jewels stolen, he was afraid Francesca would get nervous and tell everything she knew.

Even after ridding himself of Francesca and retrieving most of the jewels, Junior wanted to get those stocks back. He knew that if Frederic tried to cash them in, he'd learn what Francesca had known. Cassandra went into the apartment and caught Nicholas looking for the stock certificates.

By the way, David was following us the night of the ball. But he didn't get in. And he finally gave up on me altogether and returned to California. It had been a coincidence that he was in town at the time of the murder. But I'm glad he's gone. Mom called the other day to say he's working in an art gallery. I hope he's found his calling. Truly I do.

Harriet is helping Frederic . . . work through his problems, and I see a rosy future ahead of those two. Even Vera has been bitten by the Valentine bug. She's seeing a distinguished reporter who interviewed her about the incident at the masquerade ball.

As for me . . . well, we'll see.

About the Author

Amanda Lee lives in southwest Virginia with her husband and two beautiful children, a boy and a girl. She's a full-time writer/editor/mom/wife and chief cook and bottle washer, and she loves every minute of it. Okay, not the bottle washing so much, but the rest of it is great. Please visit Amanda online at http://www.gayletrent.com or on Facebook at Gayle Trent and Amanda Lee, Cozy Mystery Writer.

Amanda Lee

The Embroidery Mysteries

The Quick and the Thread

When Marcy Singer opens an embroidery specialty shop in quaint Tallulah Falls, Oregon, everyone in town seems willing to raise a glass—or a needle—to support the newly-opened Seven Year Stitch.

Then Marcy finds the shop's previous tenant dead in the storeroom, a message scratched with a tapestry needle on the wall beside him. Now Marcy's shop has become a crime scene, and she's the prime suspect. She'll have to find the killer before someone puts a final stitch in her.

Stitch Me Deadly

Trouble strikes when an elderly woman brings an antique piece of embroidery into the shop—and promptly dies of unnatural causes. Now Marcy has to stitch together clues to catch a crafty killer.